**Jonathan Neale**, an American who has lived in London since 1970, works as a counsellor at an HIV education centre. *The Laughter of Heroes* is his first novel.

## Other 90s titles

Keverne Barrett
*Unsuitable Arrangements*

Neil Bartlett
*Ready to Catch Him Should He Fall*

Suzannah Dunn
*Darker Days Than Usual*

Albyn Leah Hall
*Deliria*

James Lansbury
*Korzeniowski*

Eroica Mildmay
*Lucker and Tiffany Peel Out*

Silvia Sanza
*Alex Wants to Call it Love*

Susan Schmidt
*Winging It*

Mary Scott
*Not in Newbury*
*Nudists May Be Encountered*

Atima Srivastava
*Transmission*

Lynne Tillman
*Absence Makes the Heart*

Colm Tóibín
*The South*
(Winner of the 1991 *Irish Times* Aer Lingus Fiction Prize)

Margaret Wilkinson
*Ocean Avenue*

SERPENT'S TAIL

# The Laughter
# of Heroes

## Jonathan Neale

For Kate and Peter

This volume was published with assistance from the Ralph Lewis Award
at the University of Sussex

Library of Congress Catalog Card No: 93-83066

A CIP catalogue record for this book is available from the British Library
on request

First published 1993 by
Serpent's Tail, 4 Blackstock Mews, London N4
and 401 West Broadway#1, New York, NY 10012

Set in 11pt Goudy and imageset by Image Setting Ltd., of London EC1
Printed in Great Britain by Cox & Wyman Ltd., of Reading, Berkshire

# *Chapter 1*

## *(1)*

In any other country it would have been a cheap hotel room. In China there are no cheap rooms for tourists. The thin Englishman doesn't have much money left. He is travelling on his own, not part of any tour. The clerk is polite and there is a jug of water and a clean glass on the bedside table. The thin Englishman takes the room and signs the register: John Parsons. He feels tired and goes straight to bed. The next morning he goes out for a walk round the town. When he comes back to the room at first everything looks the same.

An hour later John is desperately sorting through his belongings. He stuffs everything back in the rucksack for the third time. Then he tears his things out again, spilling them across the bed: the *Tibetan Book of the Dead*, some yellow boxer shorts he used to think were trendy, his red socks, the *Lonely Planet Guide to Tibet*, his toothbrush, three hand puppets, a prayer wheel. It is not there. He suddenly has trouble with his breathing. He tells himself it is only panic. His hands rummage through the corners of the rucksack, tear around in the things on the bed.

There is a knock on the door. John freezes. His body stiff, he turns his face slowly towards the door. He is thirty-nine but looks older. He has recently grown a blond beard. Sweat stands out on his cheekbones. He stares at the door and his eyes lose focus. There is a noise on the other side of the door.

John begins to shake. Then he understands. The noise is foot-steps moving away from the door. John sits down on the bed and recites a mantra under his breath. He gets control of his legs and his lungs. Then it comes to him — under the bed.

John gets down under the bed, awkwardly pulling himself forward with his elbows. He finds one shoe. It is a man's shoe of Western manufacture, recently polished and not cheap. It is a large size. John has small feet for a man of almost six feet. Who left it? Why only one shoe?

He never finds out. The door knob turns behind him and two men step silently into the room. Each cradles a small gun in his fist.

John's legs stick out from under the bed towards the door. The older man signals for the younger to cover the door. Then he glides across to the other side of the room and bends down.

John sees a face and a gun framed by the bed. He screams.

"Lost something?" the face asks.

"No," John says.

"I rather think you have," the face says. The voice is Oxbridge, the face Chinese. That scares John as much as anything. John says nothing.

"The reason I think you have," the face says, "is that we have found it."

"You searched my room," John says, trying for an outraged Amnesty International voice.

"It is our duty," the face says. The phrase tells John who they are. The gun motions for John to rise. He scrambles out backward and stands up, conscious of the dust on his shirt. He sees the younger man's gun trained on him. The man wears rubber gloves. John knows what that means.

"Here it is," the older man says. He hands John a small ornamental wooden box. The older man wears gloves too. There is a heron carved on the top of the box. John opens the box to check.

"They are all there," the older man says. Where does his accent come from? Have 'we' trained him? "We are not thieves," the man says.

John opens the box anyway. It's all there. He goes over to the bedside table and pours a glass of water. He spills a little. He takes something out of the black box. The younger man grunts and moves forward as if to stop him. The older man says something in National Language. The younger man steps back. The older man says in English: "Be my guest."

John swallows the pill, then the water. The secret policemen watch. The older one says, "You should have told us you had AIDS."

They deport him the same day. He gets through the office in nothing flat, tearing past waiting rooms full of resentful people. The cops all wear rubber gloves and all carry guns. They are polite and careful and they do not look at him. They put him on an airliner.

The pilot's voice comes over the intercom. "Please extinguish all cigarettes and fasten seat belts," the pilot says in English. John remembers that all pilots know English. It is the international language for air traffic control. John doesn't smoke any more, so he just fastens his seat belt.

"OK," he shouts. No response. Louder: "Fastened."

"Thank you," the intercom says. There seems to be nobody else on the plane.

*

But after they take off a stewardess appears. Cabin crew, John reminds himself: stewardess is sexist. She walks down the aisle carrying a tray. John remembers he has not eaten for twenty-four hours. She wears rubber gloves and a surgeon's paper mask.

She stands a little distance away. John lowers the small plastic table in front of his seat. She holds out the tray.

She is not close enough. He reaches for the tray but it's beyond his fingers. She bends forward from the waist. Still not close enough. He smiles at her. It looks like she's nerving herself up to step forward. Then her mask slips off and she jumps back.

John is hungry, so he undoes his seat belt slowly and carefully. As he does so he keeps looking at her with a gentle expression. She has pasted a smile on her face. It's one of those smiles Oriental stewardesses always wear in the telly ads. John always thought it was supposed to mean, "Golly, I really adore giving oral sex to fat Western businessmen." Now he is not so sure.

He stands up carefully and reaches out both hands. She makes a little lurch forward and he has the tray. John sits down with his trophy. She stands there; she doesn't seem to know what to do. John doesn't look at her. She turns and begins to wobble back up the aisle. He takes the cover off his food.

"Hey," he shouts at her back. "This isn't vegetarian."

She turns. "No vegetarian," she says.

"I'm a vegetarian," John yells.

"Nobody told me vegetarian." She is crying.

They look at each other down the aisle. Shit, she's really blubbering now. "Nobody told me," she says. "Is only one meal."

"I'll eat the vegetables," he says, fast, feeling guilty. He reaches for the spoon and begins shovelling cabbage. "See, I'm eating the vegetables."

"I am sorry," she says.

"It's OK. I'll eat the vegetables. I'll just leave the meat. It's no problem. Really."

He eats quickly to show his appreciation.

She stands looking at him. She seems friendly, but she doesn't come any closer. Her make-up is a mess.

"I'm sorry I yelled," John says. "It's just that I've never been deported before."

In a small voice she says, "I have never deport before either."

John makes himself smile. She smiles back and sniffles.

"You want in-flight movie?" she asks.

**(2)**

A week later, back home in London, John's father and sister come over to visit. He takes them for a walk on Hampstead Heath. It is a spring day in 1990. The Berlin Wall came down the year before, but John Major is not Prime Minister yet and EuroDisney is still a building site. The weather is beautiful: clear, sunny and still a bit cold. It rained last night.

"I should have worn my welly boots," his sister Claire says to herself. She is thirty-five, and her reddish brown hair bounces on her shoulders. She is wearing one of her uncompromising green Peruvian ponchos. When she was a teenager she used to go round wearing a blanket with a hole cut in it for her head. John likes her.

"You managing all right?" John asks his father. Bill's wife, John and Claire's mother, died in November.

"Yes," Bill says.

"You're lying, Dad," Claire says.

"I get down to the pub for a pint and a natter most nights," Bill says. He walks with his back held carefully straight. John remembers his father is seventy. Bill's hair is white, and he still has most of it. John is grateful for inheriting a full head of hair.

Bill changes the subject. "How was China?" he asks John.

"OK," John says.

"Just OK?" Claire asks. She is heavily into acupuncture.

"Just OK," John says. He can't tell Dad about the deportation. He will tell Claire later when they're alone.

"I thought you were going to love China," Claire says.

"So did I," John says.

"What happened?" Claire says. There's no stopping her.

"Too many secret policemen," John mumbles.

"I thought they were moving away from communism," Bill says.

John feels trapped. "It's not because they're communist," he says. "Thatcher loves the butchers of Tiananmen Square."

"She's done quite a lot of good for this country," Bill says. He voted Liberal last time himself, but you have to be fair.

"You promised," Claire reminds John. He has promised not to get into political arguments with Dad.

"I didn't mention Thatcher," John says. "He did." This is not strictly true.

"I don't agree with Tiananmen Square either," Claire says

firmly. "But they do have a big country to govern."

"A big country," John sneers. He must stop this.

"A billion people," she says. "That's not easy to control."

"Control?" John yelps. He can't stop. "Control? That's elitist. Is that what they taught you at Milton Keynes?" Claire did her acupuncture studies in Milton Keynes.

Claire doesn't like being called elitist. "Leamington Spa," she says.

"Leamington Spa," John says. Claire did her acupuncture studies in Leamington Spa.

"Nice town, Leamington Spa," Bill says. He can't stand to see his children fighting.

"No," Claire says, "they didn't."

"Really lovely eighteenth-century parade," Bill says.

"Yes, Dad," Claire says, "it is."

John's legs buckle and he falls onto the wet grass.

Next day John is tucked up in bed at his flat in Tufnell Park. The worst is over. Most of his puppets are in the big trunk in the corner. Big Ted and Andy the Mouse, his hand puppet, are in the bed with him. On the bedroom wall are framed pictures of John in his working dinner-jacket with his favourite puppets. He is alive. Claire ranges back and forth at the foot of the bed, throwing her arms around for emphasis. She is wearing a red poncho today. It sets off her hair.

"Why don't you tell him?" she says.

"Who?" John says.

"You're being deliberate."

"Dad," he admits.

"Yes," Claire says, her right arm chopping air, "Dad."

"I don't think it would be a good idea," John says.

"You don't think it would be a good idea."

"No," he says, "I don't think he'd handle it very well."

"You don't think he'd handle it very well." Claire used to repeat his sentences the same way when they were kids and she wanted to wind him up.

"You remember how he was when I came out," John says.

"Yes," she says. She strides around to stand next to him. "You told him you were a ho-mo-sex-u-al, and he was a shit."

"Yes," John says.

"And now you're punishing him," she says.

"I'm not punishing him. He hasn't got over Mum yet. I don't want him worrying about me."

"You're punishing him," Claire says. She puts her fists on her hips and frowns down at him. "And don't use Mum to manipulate me."

John pulls the covers up to his neck and shrinks under them. "You gotta be nice to me," he whines. "I'm sick."

"Balls," Claire says. He likes his sister.

**(3)**

Meanwhile, in Florida:

Lonesome Snapper Pond is two hundred miles north of Miami. Agent Sam Rollins of the Vice-President's Special Task Force on Drug Misuse has rented a cabin on the edge of the pond. A shack, really. The screen doors are all fucked and the mosquitoes are murder. Sam has bug repellent all over him. He's not really a cabin man. Really he's an indoors guy, nightclubs and double brandies and impressing chicks in tank tops with sloppy eyes. He makes a mean Mai Tai.

Lonesome Snapper Pond is the kind of place that still has a general store. The guy who runs it is named Lloyd, Sam tells the rest of the office, and there's a sign outside advertising Royal Crown Cola and another sign that says CHAIN SAWS SHARPENED. CHEAP! Sam doesn't play checkers with the old boys on the porch. He has rented the cabin to get close to his boy.

He's fishing on the lake with Sam Junior. The boy is wearing the yellow check lumberjack shirt Sam bought him. You look at it carefully, it looks a bit small for the kid. Tough shit: it's the thought that counts. Sam tries. He's wearing a matching blue check lumberjack shirt. Sam's fit. He works out. He's got his gut under control. They sit in the boat. They haven't caught anything yet, but that's not the point. Sam wants to talk to the boy. He wants to sound wise. He wants his son to take him seriously. He knows his ex-wife is poisoning the boy's mind.

She denies it, of course. He called her up Thursday night and put it to her straight. That's his way. "Jorja, stop poisoning that boy's mind against me."

"Sam," she said in her tired voice.

"I got some rights here," he said. The department sent him on an Assertive Course.

"Christ, it's three in the morning," she said.

"Jorja, just stop doing it," Sam said.

"I'm not saying anything," she said.

"I know I haven't been the perfect father, but hell, you haven't been the perfect mother either."

"I don't know what you mean." Her voice came down the phone icy.

"You want I should remind you?" he asked.

She disconnected. Bitch.

Now he wants to talk to the boy. But he can't because the kid has a Walkman and headphones on while he's fishing. He has that abstracted expression they all get, don't bother me now, I'm talking to God and God only talks back in rock.

"What you listening to?" Sam asks.

No response. The kid can't hear him.

"What you listening to?" he shouts, pointing at the tape machine, waving hand signals, making a game of it.

Sam Junior takes the headphones off. Music squeaks out of them. "Two Live Crew," he says in a normal voice. Then he puts the headphones back on.

The kid hates him.

**(4)**

Next day John is a bit better, but not that much. He lives alone in a housing association flat on the top two floors of a house in Tufnell Park. Last time John got sick his friends took turns looking after him. Paul, Mark, Babur and Keith were the main ones. They developed a sort of regimental spirit about it, and started calling themselves the Firm. Claire took her turns too, but never really felt she was part of the Firm. They were careful to try and include her, of course. But she sensed something: maybe that they had to try.

Claire sits in the open window of John's kitchen, a cup of jasmine tea warming her hands. It is the nicest place in the house, thirty feet above the garden. She looks out over the back gardens of John's quiet neighbours. She feels a little spurt of anger over the great trees pollarded down to grey stumps. But on one side there is a greenhouse and vegetables, and on the other side an army of chickens peck over the brown dirt. Beyond them is a row of pines, and then the backs of more houses. Claire looks up the hill to the skyline, the great slab of the Dark Tower where the social security people lurk and the green Byzantine dome of the Catholic Church on Highgate Hill.

It's time to call in the Firm again. Claire phones Paul. He's the one who organizes things.

Paul takes the call at work. His desk is a mess, and that's not normal. Paul is forty. Last year he noticed his light brown hair was receding fast. He cut it very short and all his friends told him it made him look years younger. Paul has worry lines across his forehead and smile lines at the side of his mouth. He is a systems analyst, and his work is driving him spare at the moment.

Paul has been with the council for years. He could make five thousand more in the City, but he'd have to put up with all the yuppies. And here he can wear what he wants. When Paul feels daring, he wears his black 501s and the leather jacket he bought at Camden Lock. Of course he irons his 501s before he comes to work. The other people at work all know Paul is gay. There's no problem there. They don't know his ex-lover has AIDS. But then Paul is not the sort of man to talk about his private life at work. He still loves John. They lived together for four years, and then two years ago they broke up. Paul still doesn't really understand why. He blames himself.

And the Council is turning sour. It's the Poll Tax. First they did the program. Then they changed the rules, so they did the program again. Then they changed the rules again, so they did the program again. And it doesn't work this time either. All Paul's friends are opposed to the Poll Tax, so he can't talk to them about it. Paul is not a political fanatic like John. And Paul likes to do things right. He just can't stand it if things don't work. Recently he has found himself working late in the office, unpaid overtime, trying to get the damned thing right. He'll have to get another job. He has been here eight years. He dreads change.

And in the middle of this Paul gets the call from Claire.

Paul calls Mark and Babur's number. Babur answers, and promises to tell Mark when he gets in.

It's really Mark who is John's friend. They met at university and have kept in touch ever since. They might have become lovers. But when they met John was besotted with somebody else, and when that finished they were already close friends. Somehow sex never came up.

With Mark and Babur it comes up a lot. They're in love. They met on Hampstead Heath, Mark tells people, but not in that way. Mark was in a jogging phase, trying to hold back the river of age, puffing around in his new Nike Air. He saw Babur several times, trotting around in a salmon running suit, dark skin and flashing eyes. They would pass, coming from different directions, and Babur would smile at him. Mark thought he probably smiled at everybody like that. He probably smiled at the dogs and kids and kites the exact same way. Then one day Mark was lumbering up Parliament Hill, and Babur came running up from behind. But he did not pass Mark. Instead he fell into step, and they went on from there. That was nine months ago.

Babur came from Bangladesh four years ago. He was twenty-four, had finished his BA and was fervent with hope. His father had named him for the Mughal Babur, a conqueror, a hard drinking, hard riding Turk who loved poetry, laughter and gardens. His first two years Babur worked in a restaurant. For the last two years he has been a hospital porter. Babur hates the uniform. He says it's because it makes him look naff, but it's more than that. Mark says Babur looks great in his uniform. This means nothing. Mark thinks Babur looks great in anything. Mark thinks Babur looks great with no clothes on at all.

Mark is a counsellor. Babur thinks he looks like a film star, the sort who gets typecast as a rugged mountain trapper. Mark specializes in counselling incest survivors and people with HIV. He gets depressed. Babur tells him it's the work. Mark can't see it.

When Mark gets home Babur tells him and Mark calls Keith, the last of the Firm.

The Firm arrange to meet at John's place at nine that night. Keith leaves his basement flat in plenty of time. He walks down the Stroud Green Road, past the halal shops and the yam shops. At Finsbury Park tube a shambling white man comes up, blood from a cut drying on his brow, trying to beg with dignity and stand up at the same time. Keith gives him some coins from his pocket without looking. Keith used to just give them all twenty pence, but lately it's been more. Keith realizes he left his Filofax at home. He has to go back for it.

Keith is always forgetting his Filofax. He tells everybody his sister gave it to him for Christmas and he doesn't really want one, but what with the job and all his meetings it comes in handy. This is true: it is useful. But secretly Keith feels a black man with a Filofax looks stupid. If anybody said this to him, Keith would hit them. Or rather, he wouldn't, but he would want to. These days he has decided to be the sort of man who does not hit people.

Losing his Filofax all the time is a problem. Once Keith left it at the home of some guy he'd had a one night stand with, and when he went back to get it he was so embarrassed he had sex with the guy again, which was a mistake for both of them. But Keith really dreads leaving it at school. He never has. He knows he will. Keith is a teacher in a Hackney comprehensive. If the kids get hold of it he's finished. They'll call up his friends and breathe down the line. And if they find out about the quarter-finals, for instance... Keith makes a lot of entries in his Filofax in a private code. He can't always remember what the symbols in the code stand for.

When Keith gets back to his flat the personal organizer is sitting by the phone leering at him. He realizes he left it behind because he doesn't really want to go to John's. Then the cat yells and he remembers he hasn't fed it yet and he has to do that before he goes.

Paul gets to John's half an hour early. Claire lets him in. Paul needs the time to set up his chart. Last time they had a bit of difficulty organizing the rota. The uncertainty got to Paul. So he stole a big A2 flip chart from work — the council has lots — and that sorted everything out. Paul put their names down one side and the days across the top. They took turns at day and night shifts. So Paul had a big blue felt marker for days and a red one for nights. Then all Paul had to do was put a tick under the right person's name in the right colour for their shift. They could put the sheet up on the wall of John's living room with Blu-Tack and anybody could see his next shift at a glance. Paul plans to use the same system this time. He sets it up in the living room. John is already asleep in his bedroom upstairs. Paul knows Keith will be late.

Keith is twenty minutes late. Paul notices his easy athlete's grace, his brown suede jacket, the high planes of Keith's African face. Paul feels the familiar tug of jealousy. Keith and John were over by the time Paul met John. But Paul can never stop the feeling completely.

Claire is sewing something in the corner.

"One of the lines isn't straight," she says.

Paul looks at his chart. "Which one?" he says.

"I'm not sure," Claire says.

Paul examines the chart. The lines look pretty straight to him. "I made them with a ruler," he says.

"That's all right then," Claire says, deadpan.

They get settled. Paul thinks Babur and Mark make a cute couple on the sofa, their diaries open on their laps, Mark over six feet and Babur just over five feet. Paul envies them. They sort out the day shifts pretty quickly. Nights are more of a problem. Keith can't do Wednesdays because of his union meeting. Paul asks the room, "How about Thursday nights?"

"Thursdays is my Poll Tax meeting," Keith says very fast.

Paul does not want to think about the Poll Tax. "I'll do Thursdays," he says, and puts a tick by his name.

"I can do Saturday nights," Keith says.

"You sure?" Paul asks. Keith nods. Sometimes Paul puts a tick next to Keith's name, and then Keith remembers a meeting or changes his mind or something. Then Paul has to get the Tipp-Ex out and change everything round, but it never really looks right. Paul puts a tick next to Keith's name.

Keith mumbles. Paul checks him. Keith is looking at his Filofax. Where's the Tipp-Ex?

"I can't do Saturday," Keith says.

"You don't have to do this at all," Paul says.

Keith looks straight at Paul, his eyes white. "I know that," Keith says.

"That was out of order, Paul," Mark says.

Paul gets his control back. He breathes, then asks in what he thinks is a gentle voice, "What's the problem Saturday?"

Keith looks at the floor. There is a silence in the room.

Keith says, "I'm in the quarter-finals of the nude mud-wrestling at the Bricklayer's Arms."

"The quarter-finals?" Babur asks. He sounds impressed.

"Yes," Keith says.

"That is really very good," Babur says.

Paul grits his teeth and says to Keith, "I love him."

"We all love him," Mark says.

Not like me you don't, Paul thinks.

Quite suddenly Keith feels like the only black man in the room.

"Hey," Claire says. Paul had forgotten all about her. She's in the corner sewing something. "You want to hear what I'm feeling tonight? You want to hear my deepest reality? You want to experience the deepest anguish of my heart?"

Four heads turn to look at her. Four voices chorus: "No."

"You want me to share my feelings with the group?" Claire asks.

Together, heartfelt, happy, "No."

"Keep it that way," she says.

They work it all out for the next weeks, even though it turns out Paul has forgotten the Tipp-Ex.

**(5)**

A week later Paul is cooking supper. John feels better, so he comes down to sit at the kitchen table and chat. John has a tendency to tell other people how to cook. A lot of good cooks are like that. Paul got used to it when they lived together.

"Why don't you tell him?" Paul says, wiping the counter top.

"Tell who?" John says.

"John," Paul says firmly in his don't-give-me-that voice.

"My dad?" John says.

"Your dad," Paul says. He reaches up and takes the oregano off the spice rack.

"Oregano?" John sounds surprised.

"Yes," Paul says.

"On chops?"

"No?" Paul says.

"Sometimes," John says.

What the hell does that mean, sometimes? "Don't change the subject," Paul says.

John moves his coffee cup around the table in a small circle. "Did Claire put you up to this?"

"Yes." Paul smiles.

"I don't want to tell him," John says.

"You'll feel better." Paul doesn't know why he says this. He does not believe it.

"You remember how he acted when I came out?" John has his debating face on.

"No," Paul says. He can't decide what to make for pudding.

"I told you," John says.

"I mean I wasn't there," Paul says. Tinned fruit cocktail and custard, maybe.

"I told him. I gathered up all my courage and went home and we went for a walk and I just told him. Know what he said?"

Paul does not want to interrupt the flow. He puts the chops under the grill.

"He said..." John pauses to go into his father's voice. It still amazes Paul how John can do voices. It's being a puppeteer, of course. "Daffodils are a bit late this year. I can't figure it out: the crocuses came right on time."

"That's the greenhouse effect," Paul says.

"He was denying me," John snaps. "That was denial."

"And now you're punishing him," Paul says.

"The bastard didn't mention it again. Ever again," John says. His fingers are clenched around his coffee cup. There is a picture of Garfield on the cup. Garfield smiles like an idiot.

"He tries," Paul says.

"He couldn't fucking handle it."

Paul checks the chops. OK.

"He couldn't handle Mum, he couldn't handle me," John says.

"He is going to find out eventually." Paul hates saying this, but it needs saying. "How's he going to feel then?"

"Maybe he'll peg out first," John says.

Now Paul turns from the cooking and looks directly into John's blue eyes. His friend looks stricken. "I didn't mean that," John says.

"It's OK," Paul says. He thinks, also it's true.

"I'm not punishing him," John says. He sounds seven years old. "I'm not." His eyes are watery. Paul feels like shit.

"I'm sorry," Paul says. He wants to put his arm around John's shoulder. Very badly. He thinks John would not like it. He does not know if John would like it. He could not bear it if John shrugged off his arm.

John puts his face down on the table, his arms pulled round to hide it. He talks quietly. "When we were kids, I was ten, Claire was five, Dad promised to take us to Disneyland. I've never been so happy. I told everybody in school, weeks before. I got a special mouse hat. I loved that hat. It had good ears. We went to the airport, I'd never been on a plane before, we were going to America — we got to the airport and — nothing. Dad wouldn't get on the plane. He just sat. He wouldn't talk to me. We all just sat there like Mickey Mouse was dead or something, and then we got on the train and went back home and didn't say anything to each other, and all the kids at school thought I'd made the whole thing up. To look important." He looks up at Paul, his face blubbery. "I've never wanted anything that much in my life."

The chops are on fire.

John sleeps like a baby all night. Paul does not. He is too excited by his new idea. Next morning is Saturday. Paul is up at six, cleaning and whistling.

Keith arrives an hour early because he feels guilty about

not doing as much as Paul. Both Paul and Keith have been careful to be polite to each other all week. Paul hears the key in the door and greets Keith with a big silly smile as he comes through the door. "We're going to Disneyland," Paul says.

"Disneyland?" Keith says. He needs a cup of coffee.

"Yes." Paul's eyes are shining. "The Florida one. They didn't have it then, but it's cheaper to get to and just as good."

"Coffee?" Keith asks.

Paul stops. "I'm not making much sense, am I?"

"No," Keith says.

So they go into the kitchen and Keith makes some real coffee. Paul tells him about how John never got to go to Disneyland when he was little, and all his life John's wanted to go, and Paul's decided that the one thing they have to do for him is to take him to Disneyland. Soon.

"How soon?" Keith asks. The coffee is waking him up.

"Three weeks," Paul says. He has worked it all out.

"Why three weeks?"

"It has to be soon." Paul tries to explain why with the expression of his face. He does not want to say the words out loud.

"I can't get off school," Keith says.

"Oh." Paul hadn't thought about that side of things. As far as Paul is concerned, if the council get antsy, they can stay antsy.

"We only get holidays at half-terms and summer," Keith says.

"Like kids?" Paul says.

"Like kids. We get the same holidays they do."

Paul leans back against the cupboards. He looks deflated.

He tries so hard, Keith thinks. So Keith says, "It sounds like a good idea."

"Do you think so?"

"A cracker," Keith says. He wiggles his eyebrows. "Wicked."

Paul cheers up and straightens. "We'll have to keep it secret," he says.

"Why?" Keith asks. With Paul it's never going to be simple.

"So it's a surprise," Paul says. "It's John's birthday in two weeks."

Right. "Who's we?" Keith asks.

"The Firm."

Keith feels included. It feels good. "I'll try to get the time off," he says.

"Try," Paul says. "It won't be the same without you."

Paul leaves John's flat and decides to walk to Mark and Babur's. It's a half-hour walk, but Paul is buzzing with energy. He cuts across Whittington Park, smiling benignly at the dogs, toddlers and drinkers. He turns up the Holloway Road, with its rows of pubs for men a long way from home. Gresham's Ballroom advertises another Irish country and western singer, his pink face smiling over a shirt with mother-of-pearl buttons. In the window of the Freethinkers store the anti-God pamphlets are still curling at the edges. Paul read somewhere they keep going on a bequest from George Bernard Shaw.

Mark and Babur's house is a row set back from the Archway Road, just before suicide bridge. The grass grows high and the gardens wild in front of these houses, and some of the houses have slogans painted on the wall. Their flat is warm, messier than Paul could live with, throw rugs and kelims everywhere. Paul settles on a red and black cushion. He tells them the plan.

"Oh, wow," Babur says. "Yes." He claps his hands. Mark watches him. That's one of the things Mark loves about Babur. He's so damn affirmative. Mark has never before met anybody who says, right in the middle of making love, "Golly, this is fun." Mark cannot understand what somebody like Babur sees in a depressive like him.

"Gee, isn't that great," Babur is saying. "Disneyland."

Paul smiles. "Disney World really, but I'm sure it will be just as good, and there's a lot less pollution than in Los Angeles."

"Just as good," Babur says. "Definitely. I'm going to get some of those awful checked shorts. The ones that come down to the knee."

Paul leans forward and pantomimes looking around. "We have to keep it a secret," he says. "We can't tell anybody till John's birthday."

"I love secrets," Babur says.

Mark does not like secrets. He hated the closet. He is a counsellor. He works at bringing old family secrets into the light of day and blowing them away like ancient skeletons. Mark has recently finished writing a paper on the harmful effects of secrets in families.

"I think I like secrets even more than chocolate," Babur says.

"I love them too," Paul says.

It is everything Mark can do to keep his mouth shut.

"And I'm going to get some of those reflecting sunglasses,"

Babur says, "like the pimps wear, and the cops, the American cops with the cattle prods dangling off their belts. I'm going to be real menacing." Babur sticks out his chin. He stands up and starts threatening Paul with an imaginary cattle prod.

Paul laughs.

Over his shoulder, including Mark in the fun, Babur asks, "What are you going to get, love?"

Mark might as well say it now. "I don't think I'm going to be able to get the time off."

"You have to. The whole Firm has to go," Paul says.

"I can't just drop my patients." Mark knows he's supposed to call them clients, but somehow he keeps calling them patients.

"Of course not," Babur says over his shoulder. His face has gone hard now, no longer child-like. Babur is twenty-eight. "You're the therapist." Mark had forgotten Babur was a porter and had this thing about class. Mark feels guilty.

"Keith's really mad keen to go," Paul says from his cushion on the floor.

Mark holds his hands out to Babur, justifying himself. "They need me. I make contracts with them. It matters that I'm there every week right when I said I would be."

"Half the time they don't turn up," Babur says.

"It still matters," Mark says. "They need to know I'm there. They need the order in their lives. Some of them are very frightened people." This is true.

"You're indispensable," Babur says.

"I know I'm not indispensable," Mark says. This is a lie.

"Keith and Babur and me all want to go." Paul knows he sounds over-eager. What the hell. He is over-eager.

Babur's face lights up again. "Leave him to me," he says. "I have ways of bending him to my will." Babur flashes his impossibly white teeth.

That night, after they make love, Mark falls asleep and Babur goes into the living room to write a letter to his parents. "Dear Mummy and Daddy," he starts in English. He always starts like that, and then switches into Bengali. It is a standing joke between them, he hopes, how sophisticated their boy is. He imagines his father reading the letter to his mother, the two of them chuckling together. His father is a bank clerk. His mother is a girl from their village, and she cannot read. Babur really writes more for her than for him.

Tonight he can get no further than the salutation. He does not lie to his parents. Ever. Nor does he rub their face in things. He often mentions his friend Mark in his letters, and knows his mother will know he is in love. He believes it will go right over his father's head. Sometimes he imagines the little knot of concentration between his father's eyebrows as he reads the letter aloud, and his mother's smile hidden behind her hand. For his father Babur includes details of his pay rises, bonus scheme and overtime earnings. Babur makes six times what his father earns. Babur's father is a respected man. In the lift at work doctors look right through Babur as if he did not exist.

Babur makes notes for his letter. He wants to tell them that he may not be able to come home this summer. A friend is very sick with (?). Cancer, yes. A good friend. No, Mark's very good friend. They are taking him to Miami, America, for a visit to Disneyland. They must do this soon, because the prognosis is not good. What is prognosis in Bengali? Leave it in English.

His parents will both cry if he writes that he cannot come home. Instead he writes about his geraniums. He often writes home about his window boxes. Mummy is a keen gardener, and his father loves flowers.

Two in the morning, and John lies in bed in the dark. The sheets are soaked. He's been sweating again. The night sweats frightened him at first. Then he read somewhere that heavy sweating is how the body expels poisons it can't get rid of in any other way. That's why the sweat smells awful: it's the poison. Heavy smokers sweat at night, and drinkers, and people with HIV. John finds this comforting. His body is doing what it can.

But now he's awake and he can't get back to sleep. He doesn't want to call Paul up from downstairs. He'd come bounding in, worried and guilty and solicitous. And right now John is not sick. He just has insomnia.

It's a double bed. Andy lies on the other pillow. Andy the Mouse is a puppet, and John is a puppeteer. He started out making them. Now it is mainly performing, though he still makes a few of his own. He did buy a couple of new ones in China. It's not a very secure way to make a living, but he has always liked puppets. Andy is a hand puppet, and John's favourite. When he can't sleep he talks to Andy.

"Can't sleep, huh?"

Andy can't sleep.

"Don't worry," John says. "No problem. Be happy."

Andy is still worried.

John talks softly in the dark. "Up in the mountains, in the High Himalayas, beyond Kashmir, there is a valley called Zanskar. They threw us out of China before we got to Tibet."

Andy does not like remembering that bit. "But Zanskar, in the olden days it was part of the Kingdom of the Sikhs, and the Sikhs called it Little Tibet. The people up there speak a Tibetan dialect, and in the high pastures along the border the nomads still live in their black tents with their yaks. The air is clear and the mountains are pyramids of crystal glass. First you come to Dardistan, the land of the fairies, and beyond those mountains is Zanskar. And I've got tickets."

He feels in the drawer of his bedside table and brings out the tickets. Really there is only one ticket. Andy can travel free in John's bag. Nobody knows John talks to his mouse like this. He does not bother to turn on the bedside lamp. Andy can't read.

"Here they are. Tickets to Srinagar in Kashmir. We don't have to tell anybody. As soon as I'm over this bit, we'll just melt away in the fog one morning and send everybody postcards. They might worry, you know. Might try to stop us."

John got the ticket in a bucket shop the day after he came back from China. It was cheap, one-way.

"They have a monastery there, one of those high-sided adobe ones, like a Spanish fantasy, tiny windows high up, built into the side of the rock, and the monks sit there and sing their prayers all day. They'll have flickering butter lamps, and orange robes and those great musical horns. We'll find peace there."

Andy has drifted off to sleep.

*(6)*

At the first pond on Hampstead Heath a raised brick platform juts out into the water. It was built to cover the outflow
pipe, but it's also a good place to stand. John's father Bill
stands there now, a Safeways bag in his hand. He has
wrapped up warmly and wears good walking boots, old and
reliable. He oils them every week. He has always loved walking.

Bill looks out over the pond. He makes no sound. A few of
the ducks notice him. They glide silently towards him, careful not to alert the others. He comes here often. He recog-
nizes many of the people who walk their dogs every day. First
he notices the dog. Then sometimes he notices the people
with the dog. He has grown quite friendly with a red setter
and its woman, in a polite sort of way. And the ducks certainly recognize him. They know what's in the Safeways bag.

Stale bread, of course. And usually a loaf of fresh bread to
make up the weight. There are a lot of ducks on the pond.
Sometimes Bill yields to impulse and buys them a couple of
gooey Danish pastries as well. Today is an impulse day. One
of the things he learned from his wife was that all animals
love sweet things. It's not good for them, but they love it.
She explained that animals in the wild don't get enough
energy, and sugar is concentrated energy. Now people get all
the sugar they want and it makes them sick. But once we had
to walk all day and climb great trees for just one honey comb.
Then the love of sugar made sense. It still makes sense to
ducks.

They gather at his feet, not wanting to quack and alert the
others, but almost desperate to shout from the waiting. Bill

loves this moment, but it is unkind to prolong it. He reaches in the bag and starts to throw his bread upon the waters. The ducks begin fighting. They remind him of people.

He forgets himself in the feeding. Ducks are very beautiful, a riot of colour. But he remembers to throw some directly at the little black ones that are not really ducks, he can't remember what they're called.

A wet nose brushes his hand, startling him. He looks down and sees red fur. It's the setter. "Hello, Thor," he says. The owner is standing behind Thor, just back from the platform. She holds up a Waitrose bag. "I brought my own," she says.

The water is full of thrashing, quacking excitement. Bill enjoys himself. He takes out a Danish pastry. The setter whines.

The woman says, "No, Thor."

Bill looks at the dog, then at the woman. She is about his age. No, perhaps five years younger. She wears a scarf, the sort the Queen wears. Her cheeks are red from the cold, her eyes blue and clear. He does not know her name, and he is too shy to ask. He raises his eyebrows.

"He wants some of that," she explains, like the defensive parent of a serial murderer.

Bill looks at the Danish and then at the dog, its eyes fixed on the Danish. All the need in the world is in those eyes. Bill breaks off half the pastry. Without asking the woman he throws it to the dog. Thor catches the Danish in mid-air and scoffs it.

"You shouldn't have," she says. She does not mean it.

"I couldn't help myself," he says.

They are sitting on a bench now, watching Thor splash after ducks in the shallows. She asks Bill his name and gives hers: Alice.

"He loves it," she says. They are talking about the dog, an easy topic.

"Do you come here every day?" Bill asks.

"We have to. A dog Thor's size has to run every day."

There is a pause between them.

"And you?" Alice says.

"No. I come here some days. I don't live that close, but I love it."

There is another silence. One of the things Bill likes about her, he senses silences are easy with her. Most people talk too much.

"I started coming," Bill says, "when my son went into hospital." He gestures towards the distant tower block of the hospital. "It's a calm place here. Whatever happens, it's always the same."

"How old's your son?" Alice asks.

"Forty." He picks up her unstated question. "I'm a widower."

"I'm sorry," she says.

"Don't be," Bill says.

"I'm not." Alice smiles at him. He can hardly believe this. He has not flirted in years.

Her smile stops. "That sounded terrible, didn't it?" she says.

"No," he says.

Alice sits beside him, not looking at him, looking out over the pond. "What was the matter with your son?" she says.

He should have known she would ask. Bill cannot possibly tell her his son has AIDS. He doesn't know what to say. So he repeats what John said to him. "It's some rare sort of virus. They don't know what it is yet." It seems such a transparent lie. He waits for her reaction.

Happy dog Thor drops a great muddy log on Bill's foot.

"Oh, Thor," she says.

Bill bends over carefully, picks up the log and braces himself. He throws it as hard as he can. It goes about fifteen feet. He turns back to her.

She looks happy. His hands feel clammy. They are covered in mud. He can't think where to wipe them. He flails them around in the air to dry them. She giggles. He waves his hands madly and giggles back. Thor drops the log on his toe.

**(7)**

Meanwhile, in Florida, Agent Sam Rollins and two colleagues from the Vice-President's Special Task Force on Drug Misuse stand silent outside a door. According to information received from usually reliable sources, "Sunny Jim" Hawkins is on the other side of that door with a whole room full of white powder. Sam puts a finger to his lips. Carlos and Tony nod.

Sam loves the next bit. What he counts on is everything these days is crap. Used to be when a carpenter put up a door he put up a door. Now he puts up an egg box. One of these days Sam is going to come up against a good old time proper door. He knows when he does he's going to break his ankle.

But not today. This door's cheap shit. Sam raises his right leg to the height of the lock, kicks straight forward, blam, and the stuff bursts open and he's in the room, sideways, holding his gun out rigid, reducing the target area.

Sunny Jim is stark naked with a big piece of pizza in his right hand. Slowly, carefully, Sunny Jim raises his hands.

Tony and Carlos edge into the room. Sam takes the Miranda card out of his pocket. He reads Sunny Jim his rights. Sam knows fucking Miranda by heart. But he loves the bit when he takes the card out of his pocket.

Sunny Jim says zip.

Sam puts the card back in his pocket. "You have the right to a telephone call to the attorney of your choice," Sam reminds him.

The poor schmuck looks hopeful. The next bit relies on an element of surprise for the full effect. Sam flips his gun in the air and catches the barrel. He pistol whips Sunny Jim across the face, back and forth, back and forth. Sunny Jim drops his pizza and it gets all over Sam's right cuff. Pizza stains are almost impossible to get out, Sam knows that.

The perpetrator is down on his knees, spitting teeth onto the torn carpet. "I'll deal," he says.

"Can't hear you," Sam says.

"I said I'll deal."

Sam Rollins believes in expediting the judicial process.

**(8)**

Babur and Mark are jogging on Hampstead Heath. The run along the ponds at night is beautiful. Mark loves the moonlight on the black water and the sleeping ducks. The hill he does not like so much. Babur is good for him, getting him to do things like this. Mark knows he has allowed himself to go to seed a bit. He ignores the cramp. He counts in time with each step: one-two-three-four, following a pace behind Babur. Mark notices his partner is breathing heavily too. It isn't so easy for him either. Mark suspects Babur is a secret smoker. Sometimes Mark can smell the tobacco on him, but so far he's never actually caught Babur at it.

Babur looks back over his shoulder. "Come on, love," he says.

Mark's heart sings.

Babur is first to the top of Parliament Hill. He stands and looks out over the lights of London. He has identified all the major landmarks: the Post Office Tower, the National Westminster tower, the tower blocks in Gospel Oak and over in Hackney. The tower blocks are white, the Post Office and the railway lines have streaks of red. In the daytime streets he feels a foreigner. His flat is not a home, like his mother's house. But up here at night he feels part of a great city. Babur looked forward to this feeling many times while he was studying, waiting to leave the narrow circle of his family's imagination. Babur looks out over the dark quiet trees to the white lights and feels at home.

He wrote to his parents yesterday. It was a short letter. He explained the circumstances, that his close friend had can-cer and was very ill and needing Babur's support. As a man of honour he had little alternative but to accompany his friend to America. He wrote that he thought every day of home, the rice and palm trees along the roads and the way his little brothers ran around making enormous noise. But this is what he had to do. He would work more overtime and try to get home for the winter.

Mark is standing next to Babur. He gulps air, recovering his breath. "We are going to Disneyland," Babur says.

"I can't," Mark says.

"You have to. It is John's dearest wish," Babur says.

Claire is giving Babur acupuncture on the sofa in John's living room. There are needles sticking out all over him. Mark sits on the floor in the corner, trying not to look. He thinks he is going to be sick. Claire studies Babur's back. She holds a giant needle in her right hand.

"Are you all right?" Mark asks.

"More than all right," Babur says. There is pleasure and languor in his voice.

"You know what I've always wondered?" Claire says.

"What?" Babur asks, his face in the carpet.

"Do you think acupuncture could help John?" She sounds tentative.

"Yes," Babur says.

"Do you think so?" Claire sounds suddenly hopeful.

"Oh, yes, absolutely," Babur says.

By a superhuman effort of will Mark says nothing.

The next morning Claire looks in on John. He is sitting up in bed and clearly doing better. In fact he is in a rage.

John flourishes the paper. "Fucking Americans," he says.

"What have they done now?" Claire asks to keep the conversation going. John sometimes becomes political, and the easiest thing is not to contradict him.

"They're not letting People With AIDS in."

Claire has noticed that when John gets political he starts

speaking in capital letters. Any minute now he will start using acronyms. This is not what Claire has come to talk about. "That's beastly," she says.

"Look," John says, "right here." He holds the paper out, stabs the article with his finger. "They caught this guy in Chicago customs, found AZT in the luggage of this PWA, and threw him in the pen and didn't let him out for a week."

"Terrible," Claire says. "John..." She sits on the edge of the bed. "Do you think AZT is all it's cracked up to be?"

Yes, he does. "You've been listening to the hoodoo doctors," he says. "All that mob, they're just out to get their names in the papers and make millions off human desperation with vitamin cures. It says right here, ACT-UP did their fucking nuts, quite right too, held a demonstration outside the Chicago gaol and everything, but they still deported him, and now THT and BP and everybody are saying that they won't go to the San Francisco conference unless they let PWAs in." He is sweating.

BP. Claire is surprised. "British Petroleum?" she says.

"Body Positive," John says. He looks like a lecturer.

Claire resolves not to let John change the subject. "I was reading some people think AZT is a poison," she says conversationally.

"OK." John sighs. "People who are really sick, it sometimes affects their bone marrow. I know that. That's a risk you have to take. But it does keep your T-cell count up."

Claire purses her lips. "I think 'hoodoo doctors' is racist," she says.

"It's not." John stops. He thinks. "Do you think it is?"

Claire nods.

"How about quacks?" he says.

Claire shakes her mane of hair. "I don't like quacks."

"But it's not racist?" There is a light in John's eye.

"No," she says.

"You don't think it's duckist?" he asks.

She gives him a tight smile and wrinkles her nose. Then she looks down at him and asks softly, "Have you ever thought of trying Eastern therapies?"

His eyes narrow. He stares at her.

"Just as a complementary therapy," Claire says. "I don't mean you should give up the drugs."

John has been dreading this moment. "Acupuncture?" he whispers.

Claire goes for assertive, but not over-assertive. "Yes."

He hides under the bed.

Babur gets his way. Mark promises to take a week off to go to Disneyland. Now he has to tell his patients.

Mark loves his counselling room. In strict point of fact it belongs to the National Health Service. But to Mark it feels like home. He has never been able to do anything about the chairs. He would prefer ones with arms, and he really wishes they weren't green. Many people like green. They think green is a warm, gentle colour. Mark is not among them. But he does like the plants. There is a rubber plant and another one — he doesn't know what it's called but it's his favourite. It has big comforting leaves. He waters the plants three times a week. He suspects he is drowning them, but the third plant died some months ago and he still feels bad about it.

He spent a lot of time and care picking pictures for the walls. When he came there were two safe sex posters and a drawing of a small child in a field of flowers. Underneath the flowers the writing said "I have AIDS. Please hug me." Mark took these pictures down because he knew they would terrify his patients. What you want in a counselling room is something welcoming but not too distracting. Something to say this is a nice place, warm and safe. He spent weeks on and off in poster shops. He consulted The Firm. With one voice they said: Hockney, that'll make the gay guys feel at home. But Mark does not like Hockney, even though he knows he should. The reason is he doesn't understand modern art. He can't say this to anybody. What he really likes is Old Masters.

In the end he went for a small Monet, a house on a cliff-side over the sea, surrounded by flowers. He spent weeks nerving himself up to get a big whale picture, or maybe a dolphin. He knew it was sentimental. It might alienate the clients who had hated *Bambi* as kids. But he went for it: two dolphins leaping from a sea turned dark red at sunset. The last one was easy: a Rembrandt self-portrait, the old man's face full of suffering and kindness and the ghost of his younger smile.

Martha is talking in the room now. She is thirty-five, her blonde hair cut short and permed. She is terrified.

"You're talking as if you have it," Mark says.

"Yes," Martha says.

"You don't have it," Mark says.

"I keep getting these sweats at night," she says.

"The sweats are a symptom of anxiety. We've been through that." Mark sounds like a teacher to himself. Get a grip here. He dreads telling Martha he is going away, but he promised Babur.

Martha tears at a Kleenex in her hands. Mark notices her hands are red, almost raw. He knows what that means.

"When I tell you you don't have HIV," Mark asks, "do you believe me?"

This is the right question. She does not quite look at him. "Sort of," she says.

Martha is married. She got drunk at a party at work and gave some guy a blowjob in the storeroom. Once. Three years ago. Mark knows it's guilt. He asks, "The bit of you that doesn't believe me... why?"

"I want to believe you." Martha leans forward. "When you say it to me, I believe you. Then I walk out of here and see something in the paper and I'm right back there." She has the most amazing brown eyes. "What about the sweating? I wake up in the morning soaked. I read in that book in the library I told you about that the people who have it, the AIDS sufferers, they wake up in the morning soaking. That's how they know they have it. And I get these pains in my stomach. I told you about the pains," — she is holding her stomach — "and the thing I can't bear is this week the children have them too." She is crying, rocking from side to side. "I can't bear it if I give it to my children."

Mark lets her cry a while. He offers another Kleenex. Because of her hands, he says, "Do you do a lot of cleaning?"

"I clean all day long. I clean the whole house in the morning. Then I do it again in the afternoon. I just worry about my children a lot. I do the toilets four or five times a day. Yesterday it was five. I just scrub and scrub, I've got all the limescale off the bath. There was a lot of limescale on the bath. I really had a go at that." She smiles. "But they still drop their things all over the house. I know they're only kids, they don't really mean it, but sometimes I shout at them."

"Loud?"

That smile again. "Loud? I'm surprised I don't break the windows. I feel so bad towards them for what I done. It's not their fault. And then there I was yelling at them, and it wasn't anything they did, it's not their fault what I did, and I feel so guilty towards them, I shouldn't be shouting at them."

"What you did?" Mark asks.

"Got the HIV," Martha says.

And so it goes on. Mark tries to restrain his impatience. He always wants to rush the process. It's his greatest weakness as a counsellor. At the end of the hour he makes himself tell her. "Martha. The week after next I have to go away for two weeks."

She doesn't say anything.

"So I won't be able to see you for those two weeks. I'm sorry." He shouldn't have said he was sorry. "Are you all right?"

"I can manage," Martha says.

Mark feels guilty.

Mark tells Babur he has told his patients. Babur rings Keith and tells Keith he is the only one who has not arranged the time off yet. The next morning Keith goes to the headmaster's office. He asks the head for a week's leave in the middle of term.

Mr Potter, the headmaster, stares at him.

Keith repeats his request. He tells himself Potter is not staring at him in a racist way. Potter is staring in a threatening management way. It looks the same as a racist stare, but it means something different.

The head has not said anything.

Keith squirms in his seat. The chair is too small, of course.

"I'd like to," Potter says.

Fuck.

"But I don't think I could get it past the governors."

"Oh," Keith says.

"I'm sorry, Keith." The head picks up some papers.

"It's my mother," Keith says.

"Your mother," Potter says.

"My mother's sick."

Potter looks disbelieving.

"Mum's in a very bad way, poorly all over, real feeble like." What's happening to his grammar? He's a teacher, for Christ's sake. "And..."

Potter is staring at him. Keith can't think what to say next. Christ. An idea comes to him. No. He is not going to sink to that. He has his pride. He won't do it. He does it. He bursts into tears.

The head flaps his right hand. Keith holds his head in his hands and looks at the floor. "She's got leukaemia."

"I'm sorry," the head says.

Keith gulps. "They're trying chemotherapy."

"I'm sorry," the head says.

"It isn't working," Keith says.

The head is trying to think of something to say.

"We've... I've got to take her to Lourdes," Keith says. He has gone too far. How could anybody believe that?

The head thinks, I didn't know West Indians were Catholics. But he is too smart to say it: he's been on a Racism Awareness course. "I thought you refused to take Religious Knowledge classes," he says.

"It's me mum," Keith whines. How can this be happening to his grammar? Any minute he'll start rolling his big white eyes and talking Creole. He speaks in a rush. "It's me mum, and I'll try anything for me mum, and Lourdes is what she wants, and I'm her only son, and I can't bear watching it."

He checks out Potter. The head is staring at him.

"Her hair's falling out." He's in too far now. "The hospital gave her this wig. But it's the wrong sort of hair." That's it. Go for White Guilt. Go for anything. Disneyland is John's deepest wish. "It's blonde. I know they don't mean anything by it, it's just what they had in stock. I know that, she knows that, but that don't mean it didn't hurt her. But she'll wear it if she has to, and she wants to go to Lourdes, the priest's been on to her and she's..." Keith looks up at Potter, clear-eyed. "I know," Keith says, man to man, "I know. But sometimes you grasp at straws. You know."

Potter has heard a lot of complex, incompetent lies in his life. It's part of his job: he's a headmaster. He knows he is hearing another complex, incompetent lie now. He gives Keith the stare that works on small boys.

"Please," Keith says.

Potter knows, but what if he's wrong? "OK," he says.


The Firm have all gathered in John's living room. Babur and Mark are on the sofa. Mark is wearing his new black 501s, feeling cool and having his umpteenth black coffee of the day. Babur is having tea with four sugars.

Keith got here first this time and bagged the comfortable chair. He is drinking Morning Thunder herbal tea. He's through to the semi-finals of the nude mud-wrestling, and he's in training.

Paul stands. He feels restless, unchained, good. The room is tidy. "I guess you're all wondering why I called this meeting," he says.

They all groan on cue. Paul enjoys this. "Have we all got the time off?" he asks.

"Yes," Keith says. He is still astonished Potter gave it to him.

"Yes," Mark says.

"It almost killed him," Babur says, smiling at his lover.

"And you?" Paul asks Babur.

"No problem," Babur says. "I told the head porter to go fuck himself."

Mark is automatically worried. "You didn't," he says.

"I didn't," Babur says. He pats Mark's thigh.

"Watch," Paul says. He has their attention. He puts his hand in his tweed jacket like Napoleon. He pulls out a folder and flourishes it before them. "*Voilà. Les* Tickets." There is gentle hand clapping. Paul bows.

He hands them out, checking the names on each ticket. "One for you. One for you."

Paul stops. The name on Babur's ticket is wrong. Paul doesn't know what to do.

"She got the wrong name on your ticket," he tells Babur.

"That's OK," Babur says. He holds out his small hand for the ticket.

"I told it to her right. I spelled it for her. I knew she might get it wrong, so I spelled it for her," Paul says.

"That is perfectly all right," Babur says, hand out.

"It's Babur H-U-S-S-E-I-N, isn't it?" Paul says.

"Two S's," Paul says.

"Yes," Babur says.

"She put H-U-S-E-I-N," Paul says.

"That's all right," Babur says.

"It's one S," Paul says.

"Give me the ticket," Babur says.

"I spelled it for her," Paul says. He feels caught.

"Pau-aul," Mark says.

"Paul," Babur says.

"Paul," Keith says.

Paul looks round them. "I'm doing it again, aren't I?" he says. He is pleased. These men are his friends. They know and like him. He gives Babur the ticket.

Claire comes down the stairs. Paul jerks his ticket back into his jacket. Keith puts his in his pocket. Mark jams his under a cushion. Babur holds his ticket in his lap. He does not like this business of not telling Claire.

"I think somebody better have a look at John," she says.

# CHAPTER TWO

They let Paul ride in the ambulance. He was pushy about it, and the ambulance man and woman felt it was easier that way.

The ambulance man adjusts the flow of oxygen into the mask. John's face does not look right. His lungs grab for air.

Paul sits with his back jammed against the side of the ambulance. "I'm sorry," he whispers. "I'm so sorry, darling. I loved you. I don't know why I did it." Paul blames himself for the end of their relationship.

The ambulance man, not looking at Paul, concentrating on John's face, his hand on John's pulse, says quietly to Paul, "Don't talk now. He needs his strength."

"Shouldn't you use the siren?" Paul asks.

"That's for emergencies," the man says.

Paul feels this is an emergency. He does not want to antagonize the man. Paul unconsciously strokes his widow's peak with thumb and forefinger.

"He'll be all right," the man says. "Your friend will be OK. This isn't an emergency."

Paul wants a cigarette.

Three hours later Paul is leaning against the wall in a hospital corridor. An Asian porter passes carrying something. Paul doesn't notice what. The porter stops a couple of paces on and says, "Paul."

It is Babur. Paul had not recognized him in the porter's uniform. He had forgotten Babur works here. Paul nods at him.

"How is he?" Babur asks.

"They say they'll know more in the morning," Paul says.

"Good," Babur says. Paul does not understand how this can be good. For him it is frightening.

"How are you?" Babur asks. Paul does not look good to him.

Paul tries to make a brave smile. He still feels terrible about what he did to John.

"He'll be all right," Babur says.

Paul nods. How does he know? He hopes Babur is right.

"They can treat PCP now," Babur says. They both assume John has Polycystic Carinii Pneumonia. In the early days there was no cure and it killed AIDS patients the first time they got it. Now Pentamidine knocks it right out. Paul theoretically knows all this. He has read a lot about AIDS medicine. He is still leaning against the wall.

"If he doesn't get better..." Paul's sentence hangs unfinished.

"He'll be OK," Babur says. Babur is worried Paul is going to lose it, right here and now. He wishes Paul would sit down.

"If he doesn't get any better, we won't be able to go to Disneyland," Paul says.

Babur thinks this is completely not the point. It looks like Paul might fall over.

"He always wanted to go to Disneyland," Paul says.

"Sit down, Paul," Babur says.

Paul looks around. He sits on some plastic institutional

sofa. There are small incomprehensible paintings on the wall. Babur sits next to him.

"I wanted to give him Disneyland," Paul says. He starts to cry.

Babur puts his arm around Paul. At this point he doesn't give a toss what they say in the mess room tomorrow. "It'll be all right," he says.

Claire looks down at her brother. He seems very thin in the middle of all the tubes and monitors. The boss nurse gave her two minutes and told her not to talk. John makes dragging sounds with his lungs. The mask is still over his mouth. There is a drip stuck in his arm. His eyes are open and frightened. He knows she's there. She smiles encouragement.

She leans down close. She whispers: "Shall I call Dad?"

John shakes his head inside the mask.

Mark walked Babur to work. Mark didn't want to go in and see John. Now he stands in the small parking lot at the back of the hospital, bargaining with God.

"Please," Mark mutters. "Please. I beg you. He's a good man. A kind man, a gentle man. Him and his fucking puppets."

Mark walks back and forth. It is a beautiful night, a full moon and a few bright stars against the black sky over the Heath. Mark usually forgets the world is beautiful. Then at odd times he looks up and sees it again.

"I'm sorry. I'm sorry for everything I've done wrong. For not noticing. I'm sorry I forgot my mother's birthday." It was her sixty-fifth, she was retiring from work that day. She had to call him and even then Mark didn't remember why she was calling. "I'm sorry."

Back and forth. "Give him another year. Please. I know he's going to die. Give him another year and I'll call my mother every week. Just another year."

A nurse, coming off late shift, walks toward Mark. She changes tack to avoid him. He barely notices. Mark prays to God at all the really bad times. He went to a Church of England school. He spent a lot of his time there on his knees in the chapel, praying for God to make him normal. He would clasp his hands together, fingers laced, biting one of his knuckles as he prayed. Mark does not tell people he went to public school. He doesn't exactly conceal it either. He tells the truth if asked. But he has changed his accent to sound less posh. He hated the school. The teasing in the dormitory made him sick with anger. He fell in love with a boy named Sam. The prayer made no difference. One day Mark found himself on his knees in the chapel, eyes tight shut, praying, please God, let Sam put his cock in my mouth.

Mark realized what he was doing and left the chapel awash with confusion. He has not been back. He no longer believes in God but at the really bad times he still prays.

"Please," he says. "Six months. Let him see spring. Six months." Mark makes an offer. "If you give John another six months, I'll stop cheating on Babur." Mark remembers a boy from the Brickie's Arms, a sense memory in his crotch, the boy's tongue one moment a feather, the next a liquid fire. No. Forget it. "If you give John another six months, I'll never cheat on Babur again."

Mark looks up at the sky. When he was at school another boy told him the Chinese see a rabbit in the moon. Mark has seen the rabbit ever since. It is there now. It is a full moon, yellow and low over the trees on the Heath.

Mark whispers: "Are you listening?"

The trees are still in the moonlight.

Claire needs to talk to somebody. She can't tell her dad, so she calls Keith and he comes into the hospital. Keith has to get up for school in the morning, but he's not thinking about that at the minute. They sit in the coffee bar. It's empty, late at night, everybody's gone home. There are small pictures on the wall, mostly red and yellow lines. Keith likes them. He sees them as little jokes, the same way he sees Miro. He tried drawing Miros himself when he was at the poly. They gave him this little jolt of fun. It's hard to describe. He's surprised to find such jokes hanging on hospital walls. And grateful.

Claire sits across from Keith. He holds her left hand across the table. Claire's right fist holds a crumpled Kleenex. She is breathing normally. She talks.

"When we were little, he got so excited. He was always an excited boy. He'd dream. He could dream. He'd tell me stories. We had a playhouse, up at the top of the fields. It wasn't a real playhouse, just a gap in the hedge. But we called it a playhouse, it felt like one. He'd tell me things there, and I'd get so excited about whatever he said was going to happen, and half the time he'd just made it up." She looks at Keith. "Brothers and sisters are supposed to fight, aren't they?"

"That's on telly," Keith says. In fact he recently noticed a book in the library called *He Hit Me First*. Keith knew immediately what it was about.

"We didn't," Claire says. "You know what we called our playhouse? Cosy Corner." Her lip stiffens. She waves the fist and the Kleenex helplessly. Keith drops her hand and takes a packet of tissues out of his pocket. He hands her one. Claire takes it. She doesn't know what to do with the used one.

"Take the packet," Keith says.

"It's all right," Claire says.

What's all right, he thinks. "Take it," he says.

"No," she says. Maybe Claire means it's all right, she only needs one more hanky.

Claire reaches over and puts the used Kleenex on the next table. "When we were kids," she says, "Dad promised to take us to Disneyland."

Keith feels confused.

"He got so excited." She smiles. "John, not Dad. *I* got so excited. It was like going to the Holy Land, or being the Knights of the Round Table, Sir Perceval I think it was, and your dad suddenly said he was going to take you to see the Holy Grail. I told lots of people. John told *everybody*. It's in Florida now, you know, they moved it, but then it was in Hollywood and nobody we knew had ever heard of going to Disneyland."

Keith knows this is wrong. It was in Los Angeles, not Hollywood, and it still is, and they opened a second one in Florida. But Keith does not interrupt. Claire is really talking to herself.

"A lot of the boys wouldn't believe John, he'd made up stories before, but all the girls believed me. It was like Dad had always been there, been in the house and all, but somehow a bit off-centre, a bit in the background, only partly there. You know what I mean?"

Keith nods. He does not want to hear about this. He does not know what to say, how much to say.

"Then suddenly he was God, Dad was, taking us to

Disneyland. I got a new diary, a big red one with a lock, to write my impressions of Disneyland. I told everyone I was going to keep a journal." Claire emphasizes 'journal', making it sound posh. "We'd sit around in the evening, Dad in his chair, he had the comfortable one, and we'd say to him, tell us about Disneyland, and he'd chew on his pipe and be all embarrassed and smile, and we felt like a family.

"It was Gatwick. I've never been back. If they book me a flight out of Gatwick, like the charters do, I just say I'm not going on that one, get me Luton, change the ticket, get me Manchester, I don't care, I'm not going from Gatwick. When my friends come into Gatwick, I tell them I'll meet them at Victoria station.

"I had on this little dress, smock it was, with this pretty embroidery all over the bodice, sort of Heidi, and Mum and I did my pigtails." She stops talking, lost in the memory, the tangles, her mother's hands, their shared care in getting it just right. She cannot afford to think about her mother just now. "On the train up Dad was sort of quiet. John was out of his mind, running up and down the corridor, telling total strangers he was going to Disneyland. I held my diary and sat in my seat. I was a good girl.

"We got there and checked the bags and everything. We were early, plenty of time. Mum bought us all ice creams, we went off and left Dad, he was just sitting there. We came back with the ice creams and we sat there, just sitting there, all in a row. John asked Dad to tell us about Disneyland again and he didn't say a thing. I had to go to the loo. Mum took me. Then John had to go to the loo. Mum said, Bill, you take him. Dad just grunted. Mum took him. I went with them. We stood outside the boys' loo, Mum and me. She had a cigarette while we waited. John took forever.

"We went back. There was a noise, a crackle like those announcements, you never understand them. Mum said, 'Dear, that's our flight.' Dad didn't respond. John got down in front of Dad and looked up into his face and said, 'It's our flight.' Then John looked at Mum. She said, 'It's all right, it's only the first call. We have plenty of time.' Mum smoked another fag. She didn't look angry. She seemed upset, but she wasn't angry. John went running around the airport, banging into old ladies. Mum didn't say anything to him. I asked her if Dad was going to die. She said no, he was going to be all right.

"The last time they called our flight she said, 'That's the final call, dear.' He didn't move. John came round the corner. 'It's the last call, Dad,' he screamed. Dad didn't move. John must have been so angry, I know that now, he's still angry, John didn't shout at Dad or anything, or throw a tantrum, he just stood there and looked at Dad and realized the other boys would call him a liar and what could he do?"

Now Claire looks straight at Keith, speaking intensely, trying to make it all real for him. "After it was all over, Dad got up and walked toward the train station and we just all followed him. Mum had my hand and John in the other hand, following him, and we never said any more about it.

"And now John's never going to see fucking Disneyland."

Claire talks herself out and an hour later Keith gets a minicab back to Finsbury Park. He has trouble sleeping. Paul calls from the hospital at eight and says there has been no change during the night.

Keith makes himself go to work. He can't face the head's

study, so he collars Potter in the hall. Kids surge down the corridor, bound for classes or secret fags or the urgent passionate plots of adolescence. There is a space round Keith and Potter. No kid wants to get too close to the head.

"I don't need the leave now," Keith says.

Potter stares at him.

Potter is staring because Keith looks so dishevelled, as if he hadn't slept or even combed his hair. The man is clearly under strain. Keith is usually immaculate. Now his eyes look slightly mad. Potter guesses the poor man's mother has died. He does not like Keith. The man's a stirrer, a pushy bastard, a union rep. Of course Potter has nothing against unions as such, he has been a member of the National Union of Teachers all his working life. But unions are for representing people properly, responsibly, not for using as some vehicle for your own political obsessions. Potter does not like Keith. He does feel for the young man.

"I thought I should tell you," Keith says.

A ring of kids is gathering. The ring seems accidental, there still seems to be a bustle in the hall, but in fact fifty pairs of ears are tuned. They sense this could develop into a confrontation between teachers. This is the most exciting thing that can happen in a school corridor, short of giraffes fighting. All headmasters know this: it is part of their race memory.

Keith cannot figure out why Potter looks so funny. Potter leans toward him and whispers, "Is she...?"

Revelation. "Oh," Keith says, too loud. "No, she's fine. She's fine. That's why I don't need the time off."

The ring around them freezes. Potter draws back. He has remembered that he does not believe Keith. This is obvious on his face. Keith moves toward him, babbling, compounding the lie.

"It worked," Keith says, "the chemotherapy worked, it was fantastic, we're all so happy."

Potter makes little flapping motions with his arms, trying to say: Not in front of the children.

"Lourdes is out of the question, we don't need to go back to Lourdes any more. Her hair's growing back, you know, her hair's growing back, sprouting right out of her head. I don't need the leave any more at all. Thrown her stick away." Keith gives a little laugh.

"Good," Potter says, "great," and scuttles away, breaking through the ring of kids. Only now does Keith notice them. They look at him with sympathy. They understand from Keith's face that actually it was not that great, actually he was lying to Potter. They feel an instinctive solidarity with anybody who lies to Potter. With some of them it's general principles because he's the head. With many of them it's personal.

They look away from Keith. They do something that is hard for them, not natural. They melt away. Around the corners they talk it over, make sense of what they heard. Mr Brown's girlfriend is dying and he's really cut up about it. They feel sorry for him, but this is also surprising news. The general feeling had been that Mr Brown was a pooftah. Though several of the black kids, Daniel in particular, had argued strongly that Mr Brown wasn't, bumming was a white man's thing. It looks like Daniel is right after all.

That night Babur is working a late at the hospital. He decides to read to John. He isn't sure what book John would like, so he asks. John says *Stuart Little*, he has a copy at home. Babur is not familiar with the work. He borrows John's keys and slips out. It is only ten minutes by cycle, and Babur loves his mountain bike. The book turns out to be an American novel for children, about a mouse who is born into a human family and has many adventures.

Babur begins reading quietly after visiting hours. John is in a side room, so the sister allows it. Babur sits by John's head. His friend does not make much response, and much of the time his eyes are closed. But Babur figures his voice will be soothing. In any case Babur himself finds Stuart's adventures very soothing. He reads on and on.

Babur is aware that now everybody will know John is his friend. A hospital is a village for the people who work in it. It's one thing to be a porter who is a bit, you know. It's another thing to be a porter whose friend has A-I-D-S. Babur feels fuck them, or maybe he trusts to human tolerance. He is not sure which.

He reads on and on. Babur doesn't know quite why, but the story of Stuart speaks to him quite directly. Stuart is just like everybody else, except he is very short and a mouse. But he conducts himself in all situations with a dignity not one whit lessened by his shortness. Stuart's parents are human, but the whole family loves him, and they make sure nobody discriminates against him because of his size and appearance. The bit where the rest of the family goes out and the cat is after Stuart bores Babur: he thinks it is probably directed at the younger reader. But then Stuart meets a little girl who is fully human but every bit as short as Stuart, and his heart is lost to her. She goes off and Stuart, who has his own special tiny motor car, drives off to the north on her trail.

It is past eleven. Babur hopes very much that it is all going to work out for Stuart. It would be wrong to peek at the ending.

He reads on and on, to the end. Stuart does not find the perfect small girl. But he has some news of where she might be, and he continues north in his motor car, still looking for her. That's it.

"Shit," Babur says. He is moved.

"They tried to ban it," John says.

Babur is startled. "Who?" he says.

"The American library control people in the fifties. They thought it was bad for children to have an ending like that."

"Damn right," Babur says.

"They thought children couldn't cope with ambiguity," John says. "But the beautiful thing is, life's like that, it's a journey, a search, and as long as you're powered by love and keep on like Stuart, you don't need the ambiguities resolved."

"You're better," Babur says.

John smiles. "I think the antibiotics are working."

"It's still a naff ending," Babur says.

Two weeks later John is back home in his own bed. Light streams in through the window. Andy the Mouse lies on the other pillow. John stretches. He has his aches and pains, and his fucking itches. But today he's alive and it's magic.

The door opens. Paul's head pops around the corner, a regular cheeky chappie. Paul is such a worrier. He raises his eyebrows, meaning, everything OK?

John gives him the thumbs up. Paul smiles, raises his own

thumb and ducks out of the room. Breakfast cannot be far behind.

John turns to Andy the Mouse. John fits his old friend over his right hand. Andy wiggles a couple of times as they get the feel of each other again. Andy looks up at John.

"Zanskar," Andy says, ever hopeful.

"Zanskar," John says, authoritative.

# CHAPTER THREE

## (1)

Keith has been in serious training for the last two weeks. No Friday lunchtime at the pub with the other teachers, no beer, no snack foods, definitely no chips. He has been doing weight work at home. That matters, no question. The other day he swam twenty laps for all-over muscle tone. But running has been his main thing. Keith believes that stamina, not brute strength, is the real key to nude mud wrestling. And he ought to know: he's through to the finals.

Keith waits in the back room of the Brickie's Arms, eyeing his opponent. Neither man is completely nude. In mud wrestling both fighters wear only a jockstrap. The winner is the man who pulls the other guy's jockstrap off. His opponent is a white gorilla, slab face, black hairs all over his body, that confident paunch gorillas have. Looks like he's padded his leopardskin jockstrap too. The man takes a plastic tub of something and sticks his hands in it. He begins rubbing his hands all over himself. He's greasing himself, the fucker.

"Grease?" Keith says.

"Aye, lad," Godzilla says.

"That's not fair."

"Nude mud wrestling ain't your Marquess of Queensberry." The man gives an evil chortle.

Keith turns away. He flexes his muscles. He looks good in the mirror. Should he pad his jockstrap too? What if he loses? Then it would be pulled off and everybody could see the padding. Embarrassment City. Keith realizes Goliath has padded his because it simply has not crossed his mind he might lose.

Behind Keith Moby Dick growls: "Want some?"

Keith turns. The man is greased all over. He is holding the plastic tub out to Keith. He wants to share! He has civilized feelings, just like us.

"Yeah," Keith says. He humbly begins to grease himself. His new friend does Keith's back for him.


The Brickie's Arms on a Friday night. The disco beat bounces off the walls. The room is full of smoke: nicotine has become the ambient atmosphere. The Firm have come to cheer on their own, to celebrate, and to hold a Council of War. John is tucked up at home: they want to talk about him. Claire seems to have tagged along somehow. Paul suspects that Mark and Babur invited her. He is right. Babur gets the drinks. On his way back through the crowd three different men joggle and spill parts of the beer.

Mark's eyes trawl the room. He likes to look. He has not forgotten the night in the parking lot when he promised God he would not cheat on Babur. Babur doesn't know about the promise, because he doesn't know about the cheating. Or so Mark thinks.

Mark is wrong. Babur is a tolerant man. He knows he does not own Mark. Each of them is free to have casual encounters outside the strong arms of their love. Babur understands this. He would never try to cage Mark. Babur also understands the mild-mannered little men who tolerate their wives' infidelities for twenty years and then one day they simply leap across the room and strangle her and saw her head off with the breadknife and put her bit by bit down the rubbish disposal, serves the fucking slut right, the sloppy slag trollop.

Mark is staring at some blond God. The God stares back. Babur puts the beers on the table, carefully spilling some in Mark's lap. "Sorry, darling," he says.

The wrestlers are introduced. The crowd roars. Keith turns, displays himself. They cheer, just for him. His heart thuds with exaltation. Keith has always wanted to be an athlete. He has his game plan all worked out. He'll float like a butterfly, sting like a bee, wear the blubber out, and then...

There is a fever of betting. The smart money is on Tarzan the Terrible. Claire has never seen a man in a leopardskin jockstrap before. You live and learn. He looks perfectly enormous under the spots. The neighbouring table are offering thirty quid on Tarzan.

Babur shouts, "Here's thirty quid says the Dark Avenger'll cream him."

Mark grabs at his hand. "You can't afford that," he says.

"Hey," Babur says, pulling his arm away. "Here's fifty," he shouts at the next table. "He's our friend," he explains to Mark.

Mark cannot believe what he just did. Trying to control Babur like that. Mature people do not behave in that way. Mark takes out his wallet. "Here's five pounds on the Dark Avenger," he shouts.

Claire watches the two men grapple. They have mud in their eyes, on their stomachs, dripping down their thighs. They are tired, grunting. Keith is by far the most graceful. His skin is smooth and shiny, his muscles ripple. The other man is bigger, clumsier, and Claire cannot believe the bulge between his legs. She wants Keith to win. Friendship has nothing to do with it. She wants to see the other guy's thing.

Paul finds his mind is wandering, thinking about the poll tax program again. Over the noise he hears Mark say, "It's a pity we can't go to Florida."

Why not, Paul thinks.

Babur says, "The doctor says the next opportunistic infection will probably be the last."

Paul stops breathing.

"How the fuck does he know?" Mark says, his face suddenly twisted. "How can he say something like that?"

"I asked him," Babur says.

Paul leans across the table, planting his elbow in a spill of beer, almost shouting at Mark and Babur, "We have to go next week."

"Next week?" Mark shrieks.

"We've still got the tickets," Paul says.

"Go where?" Claire says.

Paul had forgotten about Claire. What can he say?

"Disneyland," Mark tells Claire.

Oh dear, Paul thinks.

"Disneyland?" Claire shouts. Men at neighbouring tables turn to look.

"We are taking John to Disneyland next week," Babur says. "Do you want to come?"

"Oh, yes," Claire says. "Yes, yes, yes."

"I don't know if we can get you a ticket," Paul says. He regrets it the moment he says it. He does not know why he is like this. "But we can try," he says.

Claire is in heaven. Disneyland. She misses the climax of the fight. The first she notices is a roar. The referee is shouting. He holds up each man's hand. Keith and the other man are slipping and sliding, barely able to stand up. The ref holds Keith's hand higher and shouts, "The Winna!" A cheer rocks the walls. Claire looks at the loser. God, she loves hairy chests. And his equipment — she can hardly believe it. She looks at the fighters and curses to herself, "Waste, waste, waste."

Keith beams at the crowd. This is the happiest moment of his life. Now he knows, truly knows, what it feels like to be number one.

**(2)**

It's not cheap. None of it's cheap. The cabin costs an arm and a leg. He's bought waders for him and the boy both, and shotguns, and they don't retail for seventy-five cents in souvenir shops. Agent Sam Rollins of the Vice-President's Special Task Force on Drug Misuse is taking his boy duck hunting. They are lying in the marsh grass on the edge of Lonesome Snapper Pond. Sam doesn't worry too much about hunting seasons. He bought the kid a bigger check flannel shirt this time. The kid didn't say thank you. Doesn't know how. But he smiled like he liked it. Hard to tell. Twenty-nine ninety nine. Sam hates that, the way they always put ninety-nine on the price tag. They don't fool him. He knows thirty bucks when he sees it. Plus he pays the Gross National Product of Malawi in child support every month. Which he knows for a fact she does not spend on the child.

It's wet lying in the grass.

Plus hustling Laura Smolensky is not cheap. He took her to Benny Onkom's, the Thai joint, last week, four ninety-five per stick of satay, let's see, a pig weighs maybe six hundred pounds, throw away the guts and bones and shit, that's maybe three hundred pounds of pork, and there's maybe two ounces of pork in a stick of satay, if that, that's eight times three hundred times five bucks...

"Dad," the kid whispers.

"Shh. You'll scare the ducks."

Twenty-four hundred times five is twelve thousand dollars worth of pig. Sam figures he makes three pigs a year. He spent the whole meal looking down Laura's dress while in his pants his prong throbbed and his wallet shrank. Later, both sloppy drunk, he climbed on and gave it to her and just before he came she put a finger up his asshole and it was the strangest sensation he's ever had.

He liked it, but let's face it, Laura Smolensky's a slut.

"I gotta go to the bathroom," the kid says.

The noise startles a duck into the air. No time to aim, Sam jerks the trigger. The duck flops down onto the water. Sam scrambles up and wades out to the bird. One wing's shredded, one's flapping, it's quacking up a storm. Sam takes a bead with the other barrel. He hates eating duck full of birdshot. It grates between his teeth and last year he chipped off one of his fillings. So he blows the head away.

They take the duck back to the cabin for supper and the kid informs Sam he's a vegetarian.

**(3)**

John has his first truly good day for two months. The itch in his armpits is still there, and the rash on his bits and pieces. Time was he called it his cock, aggressively, invitingly. Nowadays it feels more like his bits and pieces. He remembers a summer afternoon with Keith, the light coming in through partly drawn curtains, Keith's tight curls resting on John's lap. His bit gets excited and itches. Fuck. But his body feels good now, almost...

He stretches. He loves the dreamy moment when you surface from a nap. The four things John loves most in all the world are best done in bed: sleeping, fucking, reading, eating chocolate ice cream. He guesses that's why Paul is sometimes tetchy with Keith. It was before he and Paul lived together, but that doesn't seem to make any difference. John and Keith were not lovers long, but while it lasted John was besotted. Like a man with a glorious addiction. Keith just simply liked John. Even at his farthest gone John understood this in some left-over rational corner of his mind. That's why they are still friends now.

Paul, now. Paul he loved. And Paul loved him. But there is only so much you can ask of another person. John wants to ask everything. He wants to scream with wanting. He wants to run through the autumn leaves holding hands. He wants to throw snowballs. He wants somebody to take him in their arms and say, follow me to the gates of joy. He wants a cup of coffee. He is getting better.

He gets out of bed and scrabbles into a sweatshirt and trousers. He opens his bedroom door. At the top of the stairs some sixth sense alerts him. He bends over, peers down.

"Surprise," they yell up at him.

It's wonderful. They have chocolate ice cream, and butter pecan ice cream, and one of those Sara Lee chocolate gateaux, the kind you get all over your hands. John is in small boy heaven.

He looks around the room. They're all there. Keith, Paul, Mark, Babur, Claire, Claire's flatmate what's-her-name, another puppeteer and a singer, old friends from the biz. And Clark from Gay Lib, way back when.

"Clark," John says, surprised, pleased.

"John," Clark says. They kiss. They hold each other at half arm's length.

"How'd you get here?" John asks.

"Paul invited me," Clark says.

Of course. This has Paul written all over it. Well organized, done with love, he's remembered all John's favourite foods. And yes, there are the plastic forks and plates. When they lived together Paul had explained the merits of plastic entertaining. Some people thought plastic plates were tacky, but if you used the real thing once you got over a certain number you just had endless mess afterwards. And if you had paper plates people put them down on the floor, inevitably, somebody got drunk and put their plate on the floor, they were probably thinking about something else, and then the beet juice or the goo or whatever, soaked through the paper plate and onto the carpet and you never, never got it out.

And that sort of thing could wreck a whole party for Paul. Just worrying about it maybe happening could wreck a whole party.

John looks around for Paul. Somebody has lit the candles. John counts. Forty. All his years. Little pink candles. The political touch. They're all singing:

"— to You

Happy Birthday to You

Happy Birthday to John,"

(and a crashing)

"Happy Birthday to You,"

And a ragged cheer.

"Thank you," John says.

Paul hands him a small glass. He sniffs the liquid. Cointreau. Paul. "Fuck the pills," John says, and knocks it back.

He sits in front of the cake.

"Make a wish," Claire says. All his life she's said that. He makes a wish. He keeps it to himself. Nobody ever finds out what John's birthday wishes are. He sucks everything into his lungs and gets all the candles in one blow. That means his wish will come true within the year. They clap.

Paul is standing in front of him with an envelope. This seems formal. They're going to give him a gold watch. Paul coughs officially. Yes, definitely, a gold watch.

"From Claire and the Firm," Paul says. He hands John the envelope. It's a card or something. John opens it. Everybody watches. It takes him a minute to realize what it is. An airline ticket. He cannot speak. He's so happy. Tibet. How did they know? He holds the ticket in his left hand. He looks up at Paul. He knows his eyes are shiny.

"It's for Disneyland," Claire says.

Fuck.

"We're all taking you to Disneyland," Paul says. "It's a ticket for Miami."

John can feel the love in Paul's voice. John knows his feelings must be showing on his face. He must control it. Fuck, fuck, fuck. He welds a smile on to his face. He does not want to die in Miami. He makes himself look up at Paul.

"Thank you, love," he says. "It's lovely. It's so sweet of you." And he starts to cry. The others crowd round. John looks at his lap. "Thank you, all of you," he says. "Thank you so much."

Next morning John and Andy are sitting up in bed.

"You want to see the tickets to India?" John asks.

"No," says the puppet.

John sulks.

"You have to go to Disneyland," Andy the Mouse says.

"I don't have to do anything," John says, in the voice of an angry four-year-old.

"I want to see Mickey," Andy says.

"Mickey." John is derisive.

Andy sings, "M-I-C-K-E-Y M-O-U-S-E." He is trying to cheer John up. They sing the chorus together a second time.

"No," John says.

"It's all right for you," Andy says. "I'm a mouse. Do you know how many role models there are for a young mouse? Do you have any idea? And what kind of role models? Mickey built something. Something real. I want to see it."

"You know what Disney did to the workers?" John asks.

"That is not relevant," Andy says firmly.

"Do you?" John asks.

"You're going to tell me anyway."

"He was a fanatic union buster," John lectures the mouse. "Real trade unionism in Hollywood started with the animator's strike at Disney, and Jolly Uncle Walt never forgave them. Hated the CP from then on. Bet you didn't know Snow White was drawn by communists?"

"You told me before," Andy says.

"Then after the war, Disney and Reagan, he was running the Screen Actors Guild, they ganged up together to feed names to the McCarthy Committee..."

"It wasn't McCarthy, it was the House Un-American Activities Committee," the mouse says, "and none of this is relevant. You always get political when you want to avoid things."

John puts on an American gangster voice. "D'ja know Big Ronnie Reagan was an FBI stoolie for years?"

"They're your friends and they love you," Andy says.

"Fuck you," John says.

"And they're trying to make you happy, the best they know how."

John collapses back against the pillows. The hand that holds Andy flops onto the bed. They lie there a minute, looking up at the ceiling.

John speaks in a different voice, quiet. "I want to... to go to the Himalayas. I want to. It's an empty place, me and the sky. When you die there they put you on a wooden platform below the sky and the vultures come and eat the body. Because you're gone, you've left the body. You continue on and on. Sometimes you come back as a beetle and sometimes a man. Sometimes I guess you're a vulture. It's all one.

Because in the end, it sounds silly in words, but we're all one. You have to stop pushing the river: it flows by itself. I don't know what happens, you know I don't. But even if it's just darkness I want that peace. I want some understanding. I've walked through my life, I worked, I fucked, I made breakfast. Now I'm concentrated. I want a shape to my life, a form, a meaning." He stares at Andy. "I know it all sounds like horse-shit. But that's what I want, that moment."

They both lie together.

"That moment comes when you're alone," John says.

He is quiet for a while.

"They're your friends and they're trying to make you happy," Andy says.

"I have to live for myself," John says.

"You have to go," Andy says.

"No."

"What can you do?" Andy asks.

"I can sneak out," John says.

"I wanna see Mickey," Andy says.

"I can still walk," John says.

Andy can never resist an adventure. "Take me with you," he says.

John considers. "OK," he says.

"How are we going to do it?" Andy whispers.

Suddenly the door opens. John and Andy turn to look. Claire holds the door open with her butt. She needs both hands to carry the tray with the acupuncture needles on it.

The puppet screams.

Paul is sweating. "It's hot," he says. He means the central heating.

"It's coz I'm sick. Otherwise I'd glaciate and die," John says. He is in a playful mood.

"You always kept it through the roof," Paul says. They often used to argue about the central heating. Not argued, exactly. Paul had tried to state his point of view in reasonable terms. Then John had more or less made fun of him. In a nice way, of course. He didn't mean to hurt. Paul used to turn the thermostat down when John was not looking. He does not do that now.

"I'm an alligator. Us gators love to bask," John says. He falls on the floor, belly up, wiggling happily, hands sticking out from the shoulders at a crazy alligator angle.

Paul loves seeing him like this. "You'll love Miami," he says. He catches something on John's face. He looks hard at his friend. There are hazel flecks in the blue eyes. John looks away.

Paul says it flat: "You don't want to go."

"It's not that," John says.

"It's that."

"No, it isn't. It's they won't let me go."

"They?" Paul asks.

"They. The Yanks. The United States Immigration Service."

Not the doctors, Paul thinks. Thank God. John's pretty sick. Paul doesn't know if he's really well enough to go.

John is still ranting. "Don't you read the papers? It's been all over the *Pink Paper*. They catch any gay guy with AZT, they throw him in the federal penitentiary like Jimmy fucking Cagney, and then they throw us out of the country. Fucking Ronald Reagan homophobes..."

"I don't want to hear all this," Paul says.

"You don't want to hear it?" John is aggrieved, incredulous. He is still lying on his back.

"It's always politics when you don't want to do something," Paul says.

"You think I'm making this up?"

Paul does, actually. "No, of course I don't," he says. He gets up and begins to walk around the room.

"You think I'm making it up. I can show you." John is on his knees, scrabbling through a pile of papers by the sofa. Old *Guardians* go flying. He mutters, "Homophobes killing us and you..."

Paul takes John's wrist, stops him moving. "Darling," he says.

John looks up at him, cold. Paul kneels, still holding John's wrist.

"They're not going to let me in," John says.

"Yes they are," Paul says. "You're saying that because you don't want to go. You want to go to Tibet or somewhere. That's fine, John. That's your right. It's your life." Paul means all of this, but it comes out sounding wrong.

"I don't want to go to Tibet," John says. "OK?"

"OK."

"Look at me," John says.

Paul looks at him.

"No. Look at my head."

Paul does. He keeps a steady gaze.

"What do you see?"

"You look fine," Paul says.

"I don't have any teeth," John says.

"You're only missing two."

"In the front," John says.

"You're down to go to the dentist Friday," Paul says. "They're good people, the special needs dentists."

"That's not the point," John says.

"What is the point, John?" Paul has not taken his eyes off his lover's face.

"The point is," John puts one hand flat against each cheek, "this is thin, Paul, very thin. My hair's mostly gone. The skin's shrunk back to the bone. I look like an undead monster from a movie, Paul. They look at this in customs, they're going to see a death's head, and they'll know."

Paul wants so badly to look away. John is exaggerating. But that's not the point. The point is what's in John's eyes. Paul says, "You look beautiful to me."

John turns away. "Don't start that."

"You do," Paul says.

"Don't," John says. He means: stop.

"I'm sorry," Paul says.

"You haven't done anything."

"I'm sorry for..." Paul waves his hands, meaning everything.

"You haven't done anything," John says.

It's wrenched out of Paul. "I'm sorry I left you."

John seems genuinely surprised. "You didn't leave me. I asked you to leave."

"After I'd . . ." Paul can't think of anything specific he did. He means: just how I was then.

"I asked you to leave."

Paul does not want to hear this. "It's never that simple," he says.

"Sometimes it is. Sometimes it's just that bloody simple. I asked you to leave."

Paul flinches.

"I'm sorry I said that." John tries to explain. "I said it because I didn't want you to feel guilty."

"It's OK," Paul says.

"It's not OK."

Paul sits back on his heels. John sits up facing him. There is a quiet in the room.

John asks, gently, "Have you had the test?"

"No," Paul says. This is not true.

"I do want to go to Disneyland," John says. "Very much. It's sweet of you. I've always wanted to go. It's just I was worried they wouldn't let me in. I didn't want to spoil it for everybody."

"You won't." Paul smiles at his friend. John's being silly. Paul has heard John and his friends going on about concentration camps for people with HIV. They take pleasure in delusions of persecution. This is the same sort of paranoid nonsense. And you have to remember John was thrown out of China. That's probably what got him started in the first place. Everything is going to be all right.

**(4)**

Keith gives the American football a good kick — high and spiralling, it hangs in the air over the Heath. He runs up the hill after the ball. He loves his new Florida Flamingoes uniform. It's the real thing: he had to mortgage his granny to buy it. Keith has always had a thing for men in uniform. He does not approve of his thing. He probably looks like an absolute berk in this outfit. He hopes nobody from the Poll Tax group sees him. What if he runs into one of his students from school? Impossible. They're all safely tucked up in Hackney.

He scoops up the ball and sees John's dad a hundred feet away. The old man is walking with some woman and one of those red dogs from the cigarette commercials. Keith turns abruptly downhill. He can't handle John's dad right now. He runs downhill, loving the feel of the air rushing past him. It's good to see old Bill with a woman. He's a lonely man. Everybody needs a bit of what does you good. God knows Keith himself does.

He loves everything about his new uniform. The padded shoulders, the hip pads, the jockstrap. Narcissus isn't in it. At the bottom of the hill he doglegs left and vaults the creek, his right arm held stiffly out to snap back the neck of any tackler, the ball tucked professionally low into his stomach, hard and muscular as a wash board. Keith weaves and turns, superb open field running, look at his legs pumping, the man's reflexes are amazing, the power in his legs, his centre of gravity kept low, amazing strength for a man of his size. The crowd rise to their feet as one man. Keith goes for the goal line, looks around, he's all by himself in the end zone and he does his patented wiggle, the ancient dance of triumph and sex, all hips and contained muscle and bursting joy, forget the penalty, celebrating his touchdown and his run and his body, and little Jimmy Grady from the fourth year is standing on the path looking at him.

The little bastard says, "Hello, sir."

Keith dies of embarrassment.

After the Heath Bill and Alice go back to her place. She locks the dog out of the bedroom. Later Bill rests his head on

Alice's lap. Her pubic hair is soft and crinkly beneath his cheek. He had forgotten the special feel of hair down there. He can feel each hair, thick and individual. Her Mount of Venus is bony. He moves his head again to get comfortable, her hair brushing his jaw. He could lie here forever.

Alice's voice comes from the head of the bed. "All right?" Her head seems a long way away.

Bill purrs in reply.

"Mind if I smoke?" she asks.

A smoker. Bill can live with it. He raises his head and looks at her. "I don't mind what you do."

She reaches for the shelf next to the bed. It is solid oak, not veneer. Bill supports his weight on one arm. She takes a pack of cigarettes and offers him one. He smiles and shakes his head. She sticks the cigarette in her mouth and looks around for matches.

Bill looks round the room. It's a tip: tights on the floor, a towel over the heater. There is a picture over the bed, some kind of seascape, hanging crooked. All this surprises him. It's been a surprising day.

"Seen the matches?" Alice asks.

"No."

"Forget it," she says, and with thumb and forefinger she flicks the cigarette across the room. It lands on top of the tights. She settles back down and makes a gesture for Bill to lie on her lap again. He does. Unusual woman.

"I only have one a day now," Alice says. "At bedtime." She catches her double meaning and giggles. "I started with Al. We always used to have one afterwards." She is remembering. "Camels."

Al was the Yank she had during the war. Bill stiffens.

"Sorry," she says.

"It's all right," he says. He is still stiff.

"What happened?" Alice asks.

"What do you mean?"

"In the war," she says.

Bill is caught, surprised. He sits up, his legs over the side of the bed, his back to her. He stays there. His bare feet press the floor.

"I flew planes," he says. That's all he says.

"You don't have to talk," Alice says, and that releases him. Tears start. She is behind him now, holding him, her breasts warm against his back. It's a long time since he's been held like this. He is sobbing.

"You don't have to talk," she says.

"I never went up afterwards," Bill says. "Couldn't."

She strokes his back.

"I promised my children I'd take them to Disneyland. Years later. When I got to the airport I froze. I couldn't get on the plane. Just couldn't. After what happened."

She strokes him and he cries awhile. He doesn't suppose he makes much sense to her, but it's nice she listens.

"Now Johnny's dying, and I never took him to Disneyland." That pulls the pain up through his throat.

After a while he says, "Never made anything of myself after that."

Her hand strokes along his thigh from the knee. Lightly, upwards, and the hairs on his leg stand on end. Her fingers trail across his groin, and he feels a springing in his cock. She bends over and kisses him gently there, her tongue gliding softly along. He is surprised again. He doesn't know what to do with his hands. She kisses lightly, licks around the tip, and he's proud like a teenage boy. He takes her face in his two hands, lifts her up and kisses her, like Clark Gable, like the wind.

Keith goes home from playing with his football on the Heath. He knows that tomorrow he has to tell Potter that he needs the time off again. Before he goes to bed he tapes a message to the fridge door: TELL POTTER. When he wakes up in the morning he mutters, "Tell Potter, tell Potter." He forgets.

The next day he has to do it. He goes to the head's office straight after assembly. He stands in the corridor for six minutes. He is not putting it off. He is trying to think exactly how to put it to Potter.

The door opens. A twelve-year-old boy comes out crying. Not sniffling, it's free flow. Keith watches the boy walk off down the corridor.

Keith opens the door and goes in.

"No," Potter says.

"I know it sounds funny," Keith says. "Out of the blue. The way I see it, Mum knew all along she wasn't getting any better. I think the doctors were telling her the truth." He is talking fast. "But she couldn't stand to see us worry, couldn't stand the expressions on our faces as we gathered round the bed, so she just decided to put a brave face on it. That's what I figure. I think that's why she said she was getting better when she wasn't."

Potter is happy. Keith is the union rep in the school. He has been a pain in Potter's arse for five long years. Now Potter has him.

"That's why I have to go to Lourdes," Keith says. He stops talking. What if he brings on his mother's death by talking about it? Last time he saw her she was fine, washing windows and bitching about his dad. But what if?

"Keith," Potter says in a caring voice, "I'm not saying you can't go to Lourdes."

"You're not?" Keith feels wild hope. He looks at Potter. The bastard is smiling. Shit.

"Of course not. You're free to go. But I do have to say that if you take the time off in the middle of term, I'm afraid I won't be able to guarantee your post when you return to us."

"Oh." Keith looks broken. He cannot meet Potter's eye.

The headmaster looks at him with a firm but caring gaze. Deep inside Potter, the hills are alive with the sound of music.

"In past years I could have authorized it," Potter says. "But now with Local Management of Schools I can't." Oh, the orgasmic joy this lie gives Potter. He can't stop himself smiling as he delivers the *cliché de grace*: "My hands are tied."

Keith pushes himself up out of the chair. His legs wobble under him. His whole body is heavy. He turns and plods for the door. It's a long silent walk. Keith draws his head down in front of his shoulders. His hand is on the door knob.

"I'm sorry," Potter says to his back. Keith does not turn round. He would have to kill Potter. He opens the door. He is frightened that when he gets into the corridor he will start crying like the twelve-year-old boy.

Today is the potato famine. Most years Keith really gets off on the famine. It's one topic where he has figured out a way of linking present to past that really gets fourth-years moving. He usually asks them: where does Bob Geldof come from? They know that: Ireland. He gets them to pool what they know about famine today, and then what they remember from their project about Ireland in 1848. Then he asks them why the Irish were allowed to starve then and Africans now. Some bright spark always says racism, and the Irish kids start thinking. One year a jewel of a kid called Seamus said that maybe in a hundred years the Africans will still remember and they'll have an African Republican Army. Dot Hearns said killing is wrong, I don't care what the reason is, and Henry Whatsisname with the glasses said, What do you think famine is, and they were away.

Keith lives for such moments. But today he couldn't give a fuck about the famine. Today he's just come from Potter's office. Tonight he will tell John he can't go to Disneyland. John will say, of course, that's all right, what a shame. Paul won't say anything, which will mean: I love him and you don't.

Keith walks into the fourth-years. The noise stops as he opens the door. It rises to a low hum again when they see it's only him. A voice from the back calls "Up the Flamingoes." Little Jimmy Grady has told. The squirt is sitting on the end of the second row, grinning as Keith passes. It's a friendly grin.

Keith walks to his desk at the front of the room. He is aware that he shuffles. He puts his green plastic briefcase on the desk. He looks up at the class. He can't see them. There is water in front of his eyes.

"Now, class," Keith says. He can't speak. They wait, suddenly collectively alert.

"Now class..." His shoulders shake. They watch him now.

They sense they may have the luck to see a teacher break down, actually self-destruct. An almost sexual frisson ripples across the room.

A sob shakes him. He stops it coming out of his mouth. He looks out over their heads. He braces his shoulders.

"My best friend is dying," Keith says. "He has AIDS. We were lovers a few years ago. He wasn't the great love of my life. I haven't had that yet, ever. But you could say I loved him. You could say I still love him."

Nobody moves.

"We're taking him to Disneyland, me and John's other friends. Before he dies. All his life he's wanted to go to Disneyland. It's naff, but it's what he wants."

He breathes.

"John and the others are going next week. I just asked Potter for leave. He refused. He told me I'd lose my job if I go."

He looks at the class now. They wait hushed, like the crowd before the soldiers, each waiting to see what the others will do. Keith stands awaiting their judgement.

Little Jimmy Grady has just understood what he heard. "You're a poof, sir?" he asks.

Sue with the punk haircut leans forward and smashes Jimmy Grady hard across the ear.

There is silence. Daniel has his hand up in the back row. His hand up! He wears the same sixty quid sweatshirt and Nike Air to school every day. He is black, dark, tall and muscular and, Keith has noticed, beautiful. Daniel is not a boy to put his hand up.

Keith points and says, "Yes."

"Go to Disneyland," Daniel says, *basso profundo*.

"Go," a voice says, and another, "Go," and Jimmy Grady, desperate to redeem himself, yells "Fuck 'em, sir. Fuck 'em all."

The roar beats toward Keith, unleashed fifteen-year-old energy, suddenly let out, wild, the crowd joyous to find themselves together braver and better than the individuals had imagined themselves to be.

Keith holds up both hands, fingers out to quiet them. The murmur dies. "Fuck 'em. I'm going," he says, and they roar back. He holds up his hands for quiet again.

"Now, class," he says, "where does Bob Geldof come from?"

Claire goes over to her father's house in the afternoon. Bill is surprised to see her. Claire settles into her mother's chair and brings out her knitting. Bill offers her tea. She says no and plunges right in: that's her way.

"Dad. John and me and his ex-boyfriends are going to Disneyland together next week."

She knits.

"Oh," Bill says.

"I thought you should know." Now Claire is looking straight at him.

"Yes," he says, "thank you." Have you forgiven me? he wants to say.

"In case, John, you know... " Claire says.

"Quite," Bill says.

Bill looks at the clock. It is thirteen minutes to four. It's a grey day, pregnant with rain. The forecast was for good, but that never means much. He looks at his daughter. Claire has gone back to her knitting. What is she making? He almost says, have you forgiven me? Claire says she would like that cup of tea now. When Bill comes back with the pot they change the subject.

After she leaves he cleans up and does the dishes. Bill puts the uneaten biscuits back in the tin. Claire is watching her weight now. She used to scoff the whole plate when she came round. It's good to see she's taking care. Bill has got quite good at preparing little teas in the last few months. At the weekend he is actually going to cook Alice a whole meal. He looks forward to it. Chops, he thinks, with boiled potatoes. Something good, but not too difficult. And if he has the nerve, apple crumble with custard.

Bill knows he must go to John's now and explain why he couldn't take them to Disneyland, clear it all up before John dies. Bill has no idea how long you have with AIDS, and he can't think who to ask. He doesn't want to talk to John about Disneyland, but knows he must.

Bill has never asked anybody to forgive him before. He doesn't think anybody has ever asked him for forgiveness either. He hangs the dishtowel on the back of a chair.

Bill stands by the bedroom window. John is in bed. Andy the Mouse lies on the other pillow. Bill looks at Andy. The summer light through the window frames Bill's white hair. His face seems uncomfortable. John feels it's the double bed that worries his Dad, not the puppet. He probably cannot accept another man in John's bed, and the puppet reminds him of that. Certainly until John got sick his Dad more or less avoided the bedroom.

"Keeping all right?" Bill asks.

"Sure," John says.

"I've spent a lot of time on the Heath lately," Bill says.

John thinks of all the men screwing in the trees behind Jack Straw's Castle. He suppresses a giggle.

"Been feeding the ducks a lot," Bill says.

"I always liked ducks," John says. He remembers standing next to his dad in Regents Park, both of them in welly boots with plastic bags of bread.

Bill does not seem to know where to put his hands. He is going to say something and John does not want to hear it. Probably something about John's health. He came into the room with the air of a messenger.

"I think some of them recognize me," Bill says.

"Who?"

"The ducks."

"Of course they do," John says. Then it comes, and John does not see it coming at all.

"Claire says you're going to Disneyland," his Dad says.

John does not know what to say.

"Always wanted to, didn't you?" Bill says.

John nods.

"Should be really sunny this time of year," Bill says.

Summer in Florida, we'll fucking fry, John thinks. John is no good at small talk. Right now he dreads big talk. He knows what he ought to say.

Bill shifts from foot to foot. He cracks his knuckles. He examines the backs of his hands. The veins stand out. "Your mother would have loved it," Bill says.

So why didn't you take her, John thinks.

Bill clears his throat. His face is naked need, a plea. John knows what is coming. The old man wants to come with them. John could not bear it. It would spoil everything.

"If you..." Bill says, and John cuts him off in mid-sentence by saying, "I'd really love a cup of tea right now."

For a moment Bill leans over to the left, seems almost in danger of losing his balance. "Of course," he says. He leaves the window and walks round the foot of the bed. At the door he makes a smile. "Tea, coming right up."

John falls back against the pillows. He knows his dad. The subject will not be raised again.

Bill goes downstairs to the kitchen. He puts on the kettle with a little water in it. When the water boils, he swishes a bit around in the pot to warm it. Then he puts more water in the kettle and waits for it to boil. He puts his hands around the pot and warms them. Bill feels incomplete. He will not be able to raise the matter again; he knows Johnny doesn't want him to. For a moment there he badly wanted Johnny to ask him to go to Disneyland. Of course he couldn't really go. His fear is too great. But he did want to be asked.

**(5)**

Tomorrow the Firm fly to Miami. Tonight they are packing, each in their own home...

Mark and Babur are packing together. Babur puts on his new bathing suit and shows off. The suit is obscenely small, a red pouch in front, a string over each hip. Mark looks hungry. Babur stretches his arms above his head and twirls, singing, "I feel pretty, I feel pretty."

Claire eyes herself in the mirror. She has to decide about

bathing costumes. She has the black one on now, simple, one piece, high on the pelvis either side. Dead stylish. Claire turns to the side. Her pelvic bones don't look like the pelvic bones in *Cosmo*. They're flabby. Claire feels old. What she wants, what she really wants, is to get seriously fucked in Florida. A little voice deep within her asks if going there with five gay men is the best way to achieve this.

Keith adjusts the shoulder pads from his American football uniform. He checks in the mirror. The pads feel funny. Keith throws his right shoulder backwards and forwards, hoping the pads will somehow slide into place. He doesn't know how to wear them and he doesn't know who to ask.

Keith checks the mirror again. He is wearing only the pads and a pink jockstrap. He spent two hours dying the jockstrap. It looks OK.

He pulls on the uniform trousers. It's a struggle. Tight, synthetic, shiny, he pulls the fabric hard across his bum...

Babur is dancing on his toes, the red bulge in the front of his suit larger now, singing, "Tonight, tonight." Mark comes back into the room wearing his new shorts. They come down to the knee. There are yellow orchids on them, and palm trees and big-breasted, naked blondes in sunglasses drinking cocktails, and even Ninja Turtles. Babur stops twirling and stands transfixed.

"My hero," Babur says.

"I got a Care Bears T-shirt too," Mark says.

Paul thinks he has everything organized. He has left a list of everybody's numbers by the phone. That way he will be able to give everybody their wake-up calls at 6:45. He makes a mental note to call Keith a second time at 7:15.

Paul is standing in front of his mirror, trying on his new ruffled Mississippi gambler's shirt and straight-leg black jeans. It looks all right. Be honest, it looks pretty good. Now the bow tie. Paul likes bow ties. This one is black with red spots.

Keith will be late at the airport tomorrow. Paul just knows it...

Claire tries on the bikini instead. Do her breasts sag? Put it another way: Do they sag too much? Age is shit. Claire strips the top off and her breasts hang free. At least they're big. Really big. She could sunbathe just like this. Then a life-guard, the sun glinting in the blonde hairs of his chest, would loom above her, his shadow falling across her bare chest, and she'd look up, one hand shading her eyes...

Keith has the full uniform on now. He holds his helmet under his arm. He stands straight, like they do just before the game. They are playing that song they play, probably it's their national anthem, and the cameras linger on Keith, the clean black planes of his face, his serious eyes, his tight curly hair...

"Come on, John," says Andy the Mouse.

"It's no good," John says. He throws his new "Conan the Barbarian" T-shirt into a lump on the floor.

"Oh, John," Andy says. "It doesn't have to be Tibet. You can merge with ultimate emptiness anywhere. There's ulti-mate emptiness all around us, if only you know where to look."

"That's all very well," John says, "but what am I going to wear?"

"You think that's something?" Babur says. He turns his back and goes over to the chest of drawers, his brown bottom wiggling at Mark. Babur surreptitiously takes something out of the drawer. He puts it on his head and spins around in one motion.

It's a baseball cap, and written across the front is: Jesus Lives.

"I'll trade you my Care Bears T-shirt," Mark says.

"Never," Babur says, one hand moving coyly to cover and clasp his red bulge.

"Then I'll kill you for it," Mark says. He leaps across the room to tear Babur's head off, but Babur slips neatly back and Keith ends up clutching him lower down, around the waist, his open mouth falling towards...

On the beach, the blond lifeguard slowly slides Claire's bikini bottom off. "Why, mam," he says, his voice liquid molasses, "I don't believe I've ever met a real woman as purty as you." His teeth shine. Claire reaches for his surfer trunks...

John takes a small pair of wraparound reflecting sunglasses from his bedside table. He places them gently on Andy's face. The mouse chokes back a sob of gratitude. John smiles at him.

"Buddy," Andy says.

"Yeah?"

"Thanks," Andy says.

John produces another pair of reflecting shades, larger, more menacing. John puts them on his own face. They get up and walk over to the mirror on the closet door.

"Dead cool, Kemo Sabe," Andy says.

"Something, huh?" John says.

They admire themselves for a time.

"We're gonna see Mickey," Andy says. John feels happy for the little critter.

# *Chapter 4*

## *(1)*

The plane is full of young English couples wearing colourful T-shirts and pale Yorkshire faces. When they land the young ones break lanes and stream off down the corridor, hustling for position. This crowd are experienced packagees: they know about immigration lines. Babur hustles right along with them. He looks around for Mark. Mark is not there. Babur looks back.

His friends are way down the corridor. John is tottering. He leans on Paul's arm. He looks very thin. Babur stands and waits for them. He controls his impatience. They almost drag John up to Babur.

"They'll find the AZT," John says.

"Don't be silly," Paul says. John is being paranoid again.

"I think they will look for it," Babur says. Looking at John, he knows they will.

Paul looks betrayed.

"Give it to me," Babur says to John.

"It's in the bag," John says. Paul is carrying John's silver Head bag. Babur takes the bag from him. Then Babur sees the policewoman. She is stands motionless by the Coke machine, ten feet away, her back to the wall. The cop has watched the whole thing. She wears a short black skirt and a holster on her belt. The gun hangs down below the hem of her skirt. Babur holds the bag uncertainly, letting it swing. He is tempted to run.

Claire, busy, sure, takes her brother's bag from Babur's hand and unzips it. She tumbles through the contents, muttering, "Men are such pigs." Andy's face pops up briefly and then disappears back into the bag. "Gotcha," Claire says, and pulls out a black box. She looks at John to check it's the right box.

"Aargh," John says, "Kryptonite," and throws his hands up to shield his face.

Babur sneaks a look at the policewoman. She is still there. She has seen the whole thing. She is chewing gum.

Claire jams the black box into her shoulder bag. She says to Babur, in what she imagines is a conspiratorial whisper, "I thought they were more likely to search you." Everybody in the queue turns to look. "Racism, you know," Claire bellows.

Babur feels offended. He knows this is unfair. "They're more likely to search you," he whispers, "hippy."

"I can't hear you," Claire says.

The whole queue is watching. One young married points at Babur and says something to the Gazza clone with her. Babur leans close to Claire and whispers in her ear: "Hippy."

They form one long line for passport control. At the front of the line a man in short hair and a blue suit directs them to different booths as they become available.

Mark is first at the passport desk. The man glances at his picture and waves him through.

Claire shambles to the desk, three bags over her left shoulder and a plastic Duty Free bag in her hand. The man at the desk looks up. Claire looks back at him. They lock glances. She senses he is waiting for some sign from her. She can't tell what. "Passport," he says.

"Oh," she says, giving a slightly guilty laugh, scrabbling through her bags. "It's in here somewhere," she says.

"That's OK, lady," he says. "I got all day."

She finds it. He stamps it. She is through. Customs is next. Claire clutches at the bag with the AZT and tries to look nonchalant. She strides out, her bags banging against the top of her hip.

Babur is next. The woman behind his desk has a blue rinse. She looks like a mum to Babur. He gives her a warm smile. She stamps his passport without a word.

Keith goes through right behind Babur. The woman looks at his passport picture. She turns it upside down and looks at it again. "Middle name?" she says.

Why are they doing this to me, Keith asks himself, as if he didn't know.

"Middle name?" she says.

"Erasmus," Keith says. He has not forgiven his mother.

"Date of birth?" she says. This is going to take a while.

Paul and John are left. The man motions Paul forward. John takes his hand off Paul's elbow and walks toward the booth. The dictator in the blue suit puts out a hand to stop Paul.

"I'm with my friend," Paul says, keeping his voice tight and polite.

The suit nods. Paul follows John, who seems to be dragging his legs along the floor. They reach the booth. The man behind the desk smiles at them, happy, not friendly.

"What have we here?" the man asks.

Claire and Babur are standing amidst their bags outside Arrivals. It's hot, for English people almost unbelievably hot. By Claire's watch they have been waiting eleven minutes. Mark has changed some money and gone off to get them all Diet Cokes.

Keith comes out of Arrivals, looking hassled. He sees them and smiles. He looks around and stops smiling. As he comes up to them he says, "Where's John?"

"Not here yet," Claire says. She taps her toe.

Claire's watch says sixty minutes. She is reasonably sure. "We better find out what happened to them," she says.

"How?" Mark asks.

"Ask," Claire says.

"Won't that call attention to them?" Mark asks.

"It'll show they have some friends," Claire says.

She walks towards the arrival doors. A policeman stops her. She asks him something.

John is in a wheelchair. The heat comes up off the tarmac and pummels him. He did not sleep much on the plane. He lolls back against the wheelchair. A cop pushes the chair. John looks up at the cop's face.

"I could spit in your eye," John says. The cop's head jerks back involuntarily.

The fuckers are deporting him.

Again.

Paul is handcuffed to the wheelchair. He won't let them

see a gay man cry. When he gets home he will sit down and weep for all his hopes and plans and dreams. Not here. Paul blames himself. He should have known this would never work. John told him. He just didn't listen.

"If I gotta go, bluebottle, I'm gonna take ya wid me," John says to the policeman pushing the wheelchair.

"Please, John," Paul says.

"It's the only language they understand," John hisses.

The policeman ignores John.

It's all Paul's fault.

**(2)**

An hour later Claire, Babur, Mark and Keith are sitting on their luggage in the arrivals lobby, glum. They know John is being deported.

"So what do we do?" Babur asks nobody in particular.

"We'll have to go back to London," Keith says. Back to school, he thinks, shit. He needs a drink.

"No," Claire says loudly.

The others look startled.

"No," Claire says. "We're not going back. We're going to Disneyland."

Keith thinks this is over the top. Just because she didn't get to Disneyland when she was little doesn't mean she should forget John.

"I don't want to go to Disneyland," Mark says.

"You don't?" Keith asks. Paul had been quite categorical about Mark and Babur both being mad keen for Disneyland.

"No," Mark says, tired.

"Because of what's happened to John?" Keith asks Mark.

"I never wanted to go to Disneyland," Mark says. He sounds bitter.

"Oh," Keith says. He ponders. "Me neither," he says.

"You didn't want to go to Disneyland?" Babur asks Mark. He looks disappointed.

"No." Mark shakes his head.

"Oh," Babur says. He slumps on his suitcase, purses his lips, looks at his hands.

"We're going to Disneyland and we're taking John and Paul," Claire says decisively.

Mark and Keith just look at her. Babur smiles at her and says, "How?"

Their motel has a small kidney-shaped swimming pool, a pay phone and a Coke machine. Babur and Mark are swimming in their new bathers. Babur splashes Mark. Mark does not splash back. He feels that in the circumstances it would not be right to have too much fun.

Claire has armed herself with a fistful of the funny small American change. She rings the same number she has been trying all day. It rings and rings. Maybe it takes a long time to get to the phone.

Claire holds the phone in her left hand and drums her right fist against the dark plastic hood of the pay phone. "Answer, damn you, answer," she says.

Claire realizes she has John's AZT.

"OK?" Paul asks for the thousandth time.

"OK," John says. He feels terrible. He's in a courtesy wheelchair from the airline. They're back at Heathrow.

They got through customs. The fuckers couldn't keep him out of his own country. They haven't found the bags. God alone knows what planet they've sent the luggage to. Paul is pushing him.

"I'm sorry," Paul says.

John doesn't have the energy to reassure Paul again.

"I thought you were paranoid," Paul says.

"I thought I was paranoid too," John says.

John got some sleep on the plane, but not enough. His legs hurt. He doesn't know why. He rests his eyes.

Paul says, "Good Lord."

John opens his eyes. His father is standing in front of him.

"I've got three tickets for the Bahamas, leaving in forty-five minutes. Can you do it?" Bill asks.

John just stares at his Dad. Bill shows them the tickets. "Claire called me," Bill says. There is a wild smile in his eyes.

He knows everything, John thinks.

"Are you up to the Bahamas?" Bill asks.

John nods. Pretty soon he'll be able to speak.

"You certain?" Bill asks.

"Yes," John says. Why the Bahamas? he thinks.

Bill is already leading the way across the airport. Paul follows in his wake, the chair veering from side to side. Paul is not very good at pushing it yet. Paul catches up, falls into step beside Bill.

"Why the Bahamas?" Paul asks.

"I can fly from there," Bill says. He looks like David Niven on speed.

Of course, John thinks, Dad'll fly me. He goes to sleep.

They make the Bahamas plane with twenty minutes to spare. They sit together in a non-smoking section. Paul offers Bill the window seat. The old man firmly refuses. They shook John awake for boarding but he's gone back to sleep. Paul knows John is fine now. With any luck they will be in Disneyland the day after tomorrow. The sign comes on and Paul does up John's seat belt.

Bill is in the aisle seat. He leans across John to ask Paul, "Do you think they have any of those little bags?"

The old man does not look well. "What bags?" Paul says.

"Sick bags," Bill says. The old man seems to be clenching his teeth. His hand grips the arm rest like a claw.

"Sick bags," Paul murmurs. "I think so." He looks through the little hammock in front of him. In-flight magazine, duty-free price list, safety instruction cards. Paul wonders where the inflatable life preserver is. No sick bag.

"Doesn't appear to be one," Paul says. Bill is staring straight ahead. The engines throb, revving for takeoff. Bill does not look good. Paul's little brother Ed used to look just like that on long car journeys before he... "Oh, dear," Paul says.

Paul takes his carry-all from under the seat. He rifles through it, finds the Marks and Sparks bag full of his new underwear. The bag is small and green. It looks just the ticket. His underwear will be perfectly all right in with the other clothes. He empties the plastic bag and hands it to Bill.

Bill's head is locked front. He thanks Paul with a curt nod.

The engines rev louder. Bill carefully lowers his mouth to the opening of the bag.

Paul remembers that the awful thing is that each time he never even felt carsick until after Ed threw up.

John's sleep is disordered. He knows he has a fever. He has snatches of dreams, phantasmagoric. He has no strength for a plot line, only images. He sees the grim reaper, and banshees, and the frightened mother from a Kathe Kollwitz lithograph, clutching her children and Kermit the Frog. Kermit comes into the dream several times. John hero-worships Kermit. Andy is telling Kermit it will be all right, Dad's here to take care of us, and Kermit says in the voice of doom, the voice of a gypsy fortune-teller, "Don't trust Dad." And there are the Four Horsemen of the Apocalypse on their steeds, their ghastly cloaks billowing about them, Mickey, Donald, Goofy and their leader Milarepa. Milarepa, the macho trickster, the hermit of Mount Kailas, the monk who brought Buddhism to Tibet, with his karate kicks and his song battles with the priests of the old Bon religion. The four horsemen laugh atop their steeds and ride over Kermit and Andy, ride them into the hard dust of Tibet. And as he goes under the hooves Andy looks around for John, eyes wide, but John cannot help him. He is too sick to move.

"It's been a long day," Bill says. He feels old.

"Yes," Paul says. The Captain's Cabin is air conditioned, a blessed relief from the streets of Freetown in September. Paul and Bill have a glass of Bud each: Bill's third, Paul's fourth. They are trapped in the Bahamas.

"We fucked up," Paul says.

"Quite," Bill says.

They both think about John back at the hotel.

"Do you think he's all right?" Bill asks.

Paul drains his glass. "No," he says. He slaps the glass down on the table.

"How important is the A-Zed-Bee?" Bill asks.

Paul does not bother to correct him. "He says it's not that important. It's just long-term use."

"I don't understand," Bill says.

"It doesn't cure the things he gets, the infections. It just props up the underlying immune system."

Bill rubs the bridge of his nose with his thumb and forefinger. "He's getting worse," he says.

"Yes," Paul says.

"Because we brought him here."

"Probably," Paul says. He picks up his empty beer glass and looks at the drops moving on the bottom. "Barrel of laughs, guilt," he says.

"I didn't think," Bill says. "I just assumed I could rent a plane and fly over. I didn't think they'd ask for a licence." Bill was badly humiliated at the airfield today. At the first office the girl was young and brown and pretty, and he actually told her he flew Spitfires in the war. She turned suddenly kind, pity on her face. After that he and Paul trudged from office to office, going through the motions, expecting nothing.

"But can you fly?" Paul says.

For a moment Bill is irritated. Then he realizes Paul means no harm. "Oh sure," Bill says. "No problem. Be happy." He tips back his beer.

"We could get a boat," Paul says for the eleventh time.

"No," Bill says. "It's too far. Johnny wouldn't make it." They would need to get one of those small cigarette boats to sneak past the coastguard. The waves would shake hell out of it. Bill has explained this to Paul five times.

"Want another one?" Paul asks.

"Of course," Bill says.

Paul goes to the bar. The man at the next table stands up, walks over and leans his hands on the chair next to Bill. The man is big, white, overweight but not really fat. He wears a short-sleeved shirt and a green tie. His hair is red, his face freckled. He holds out a sunburned arm. "Dwayne, sir." He does not give his last name. "I couldn't help eavesdropping on your conversation." The voice is Southern.

Bill nods at the chair. Dwayne pulls it out, hunkers down and says, "You appear to be a pilot without a plane. Am I right?"

"Right," Bill says. He may be drunk, but he is not naive. He knows where this is heading.

"And I, in a manner of speaking, am a plane without a pilot," Dwayne says.

That was where Bill thought this was heading. "Pleased to meet you," he says.

"Yes," Dwayne says. He looks around the room. He leans toward Bill. His piggy eyes smile. "And am I right in thinking that you want to import into the United States of America a person or persons who might be interdicted by the United States Immigration and Naturalization Service?"

"My son," Bill says.

"I'm sorry to hear that," Dwayne says.

Bill acknowledges with a nod.

Paul is there with the beers. He stops.

"Paul," Bill says, "this is Dwayne. He has a plane." Bill looks hard at Paul, telegraphing: Don't Ask. "Dwayne, this is my son's friend Paul."

Dwayne holds out a freckled ham. "Pleased to meet you."

They sit. And then for half an hour they make small talk. Bill supposes that is how these things are done. Dwayne comes back with another round of beers.

"Pardon me asking, sir, but what ever happened to your pilot's licence?" Dwayne says.

"Angola," Bill says. "Seventy-eight. They took it off me after that." If he believes that he'll believe anything.

"Angola." Dwayne rolls the syllables around his mouth, weighing this old man up anew. He is impressed.

This is bad, what Bill is getting into, very, very bad. He has no illusions about what will be in Dwayne's plane. But he has to get Johnny to Disneyland.

Two beers later they shake on the deal and stagger out of the Captain's Cabin. At the table behind them a white man has passed out, the side of his face resting in a beer spill. The Captain's Cabin is the sort of place they don't hassle you.

Now the white man raises his head and comes alive. He reaches into his trouser pocket for a hanky and wipes his face. He goes across to the pay phone by the gents and makes a credit card call.

A cool bored female voice answers: "Can I help you?"

"Gimme Sam Rollins," 'Sunny Jim' Hawkins says.

"Whom shall I say is calling?" she asks.

"What are you, fresh off the boat?"

Special Agent Sam Rollins comes on the line. "Yes?"

"Sam?"

"Yeah."

"This is Sunny Jim here. I got a hot one for you."

Sam Rollins can't stand Sunny Jim. But given the nature

of his work Sam has little choice but to rely on informers. So Sam Rollins listens. Then he puts the phone down and moves into action.

**(4)**

Mark, Babur and Claire are sitting by the motel pool with their shades on drinking Cokes. Keith is walking around the pool in his white 501s and his white "Young Marlon" T-shirt. The white sets off the black of his skin, and he knows it. He is dressed to kill with no place to go. He is also manic. He hates waiting.

"I hate waiting," Keith says.

"Have a Coke," Babur says.

Keith shakes his head and keeps pacing.

The old bloke at reception comes out and says there's a call for Claire Parsons. She runs for the phone. It's her dad.

She comes back and tells the others her dad has found a nice man who has agreed to fly him and Paul and John to Florida in his plane. They're all supposed to meet tomorrow night at the Valhalla Motel in some place called Lonesome Snapper. Claire is almost squealing with happiness. Keith is relieved. He has a Coke.

Claire, Mark and Babur head off to find a car rental place. Keith has to trade, and when he has to trade, he has to trade. He promises to meet them in Lonesome Snapper tomorrow night.

The car hire people don't know where Lonesome Snapper is either, but they look it up. Mark calls his patient Martha back in London and leaves a message on the answering machine. Babur sends his mother a postcard of dolphins playing in the water. He tells her that America is very hot but he is having a nice time.

Keith stands at the bar in Oz East. The place is packed. Men can hardly move. A white giant in a black T-shirt shoves his way to the bar. He arrives next to Keith. The giant holds out a paw full of money for the barman. He glances at Keith. He looks again. "Howdy," he says. Really: howdy.

"Hello," Keith says.

"You English?" Surprised.

"Yes," Keith says. He does not often think of himself as English, but of course he is.

"Thought so. Yawl have the cutest accent," the giant says. Such muscles. He seems to have forgotten the barman. He reads Keith's face. "I'm sorry. You probably hate me for saying that." He makes a face like a little boy who has been very bad.

"I think your accent's real cute too," Keith says. The biceps.

The giant smiles. Even his teeth are enormous. Keith wonders...

"Want a drink?" the giant asks.

"Yes please." Keith feels like a kid. He likes the feeling. "I'm Keith."

"I'm Zeke."

They smile at each other.

"What?" Zeke asks.

"What what?" Keith says.

"What are you drinking?" Zeke says.

"Surprise me," Keith says.

They take Zeke's car. On the way home Zeke asks, "What do you do?"

"For a living?" Keith says.

"Yeah."

"I'm a teacher." Then Keith corrects himself. "I used to be a teacher. I don't know if I have a job now. Don't really know what I am."

"Sounds rough," Zeke says, driving one-handed.

"Yeah," Keith says. "I'll make it." He squirms back in his seat. He revels in Zeke's car. It's not just a big black car with smoked windows: it's a major ecological crime.

"What do you do?" Keith asks.

Keith runs his hand across Zeke's chest. The hair is blond, curly, almost tangled. Keith trails his fingers lightly through it. He can see Zeke's pectorals slide under the chest hair. Soon it will be time for them to do it again. Now? He leans over and begins gently tonguing around the edges of Zeke's nipple.

"What's a nice guy like you doing in a place like this?" Zeke asks.

Keith stops. "In your bed?"

"Nah. I know what you're doing here. Keep doing it. What are you doing in Florida?"

Keith tells him.

"That's the sweetest story I ever heard," Zeke says.

"It's his dearest wish," Keith says, as if that explains everything.

"That's so sweet," Zeke says. For a moment he seems lost. Then he sits up fast, bouncing Keith off. "What's your dearest wish, my sweet man?" he asks.

Keith gestures.

"No, not that," Zeke says. "Seriously. What's your deepest wish?"

"Uh- tu- tu-" Keith splutters. He cannot say it.

The white giant picks up a pillow. "Talk, or I'll beat it out of you."

Keith hides his head under the other pillow.

"Talk, varlet," Zeke shouts, and begins pounding Keith with the pillow. Zeke uses maybe a twentieth of his strength.

Keith giggles.

"Talk. Tell me your deepest wish."

The giggle is uncontrollable.

Keith takes the pillow off his head and begins hitting back with it. The room fills with feathers. Much later, Keith tells Zeke his deepest wish.

*(5)*

It is dusk on a small cay in the Bahamas. Paul and John strap themselves into the back seats of the small plane. John looks better. Paul is certain of that. John did not want to see a doctor, but they overrode him this morning and had the quack in. Now John is covered with anti-fungals and full of antibiotics and painkillers. He looks tired, yes, but he'll make it.

Paul is very surprised that Bill is doing this. There are sacks and sacks of something in the back of the plane. Paul is not even sure what. He cannot imagine what will happen to them if they're caught. He does not like Dwayne, the cracker in the suit. Paul takes John's hand. "It'll be all right," Paul says.

"Too right," John says.

Up front Bill appears to be inspecting the controls. Paul hopes the old man knows what he's doing. He hopes, for instance, that instrument panels have not changed much in the last fifty years. The cracker in the suit has the other front seat.

"You sure you know what you're doing?" Dwayne asks Bill.

Bill does not answer. Instead, he turns something on and the engines start making a noise. The old man seems just to be listening to the noise. Paul is not at all sure he can fly.

"What bearing?" Bill says.

Dwayne scrambles to consult the map. "291," he says.

The old man eases something forward and suddenly they're moving. The dirt airstrip thuds and bumps past Paul. He does not like small planes. There are trees at the end of the airstrip, palms, coming right at Paul. With a lurch they are above the trees and climbing steeply, Paul pressed back into his seat. Two minutes later they are flying a flat trajectory, tiny white caps flecking the sea way below, and Paul breathes. He eases his grip on John's hand. John winks at him. "I love you," Paul says.

Bill vomits all over the controls. Dwayne twists in his seatbelt. "Barf," he exclaims.

Bill looks at the control panel sadly.

Paul checks. It's OK. Bill still has his hands on the controls. The plane is still flying straight.

"I'm terrible sorry," Bill says.

"That's OK," Paul says. "I've got a hanky."

"Are you all right?" Dwayne asks Bill.

"Right? Oh, yes. Quite. Perfectly all right," Bill says. "Touch of fear," he confides.

"Touch of fear?" Dwayne asks.

"Yes. Get it every time. Nothing to worry about." Bill takes a hanky from Paul. "Sorry to ask this, Dwayne, but do you think you could just..."

Bill holds out the hanky. Dwayne shrinks.

"I have to fly the plane, you see," Bill says.

Dwayne takes the hanky. He looks at the mess on the controls. He looks at the hanky. It's a small hanky.

"You all right back there, Johnny?" Bill calls.

"Yo," John says. He is enjoying himself.

**_(6)_**

Meanwhile, in Lonesome Snapper:

Special Agent Sam Rollins of the Vice-President's Task Force on Drug Misuse has hit a wrinkle. Dwayne and the English connection appear to have confederates already installed at the Valhalla Motel. Sam is outside the motel room with two colleagues now. Another one is covering the front desk. The desk clerk said an Asian male, a Caucasian male and a Caucasian female. Who knows what they're up to by now. Sam hopes it's dirty.

He nods to Tony and Carlos. He can't kick the door down this time. The busted door would give the game away when the others come. Sam misses it, but you have to live in the real world. He turns the door handle silently, snaps the door open "Bang" and leaps into the room. "Drop your cocks and grab the sky," he shouts.

Mark, Babur and Claire grab the sky. They have seen the movies too.

"This is a stake-out," Sam says. He really gets off on saying that.

**(7)**

Half an hour out of the Bahamas, John and Paul are talking quietly together in the back seat of the plane.

"I had a test," Paul says.

"I thought you didn't," John says.

"I told you I didn't," Paul says.

"Oh."

"It was negative," Paul says.

"Why didn't you tell me?"

Paul finds he cannot explain this. He did not feel happy when they told him the result. He should have felt happy. Or at least relieved. Instead Paul felt guilty. He felt he had betrayed John, left him. Paul wanted both of them to face it together, hand in hand. He didn't want to be Florence Nightingale and the legless lieutenant, he wanted to be Butch Cassidy and the Sundance Kid. He did not want to pity John. Paul doesn't know how to say any of this to John. Partly he's not good with words. Partly it all feels a bit crazy, and Paul doesn't like being crazy. He turns to explain all this mess. John has gone to sleep.

In the pilot's seat Bill has been listening to the conversation behind him. He is astonished. He presumes Paul meant an AIDS test. He had always assumed that John got it from Paul. He has been polite to Paul all along. That was how Bill was brought up, and he happens to think politeness matters. But he has hated Paul for what happened to Johnny. Now he doesn't know what to think. If it wasn't Paul, who was it? How many were there? This must mean Johnny and Paul thought John had given it — the virus — to Paul. And why didn't Paul get it from Johnny? There is an image in Bill's mind, a man's long penis sinking into Johnny's bottom. He shuts his eyes hard to get rid of the picture.

"Wake up," Dwayne says quietly.

"Sorry," Bill says.

"Your boy's got AIDS, hasn't he?" Dwayne asks.

"Yes," Bill says. Saying it is a relief. "It's not catching. Not like this, I mean."

"I know," Dwayne says. There is something in his voice. Bill turns his head to look directly at the American.

"We, uh, the AIDS virus is pretty common in the drug-using community in Florida at this point in time," Dwayne says.

Bill looks through the windshield at the night sky again. He is thinking about what is in the back of the plane. Actually, this is insane. He cannot imagine how he got here, with his son with... and a whole plane full of... and some fat spiv in a green tie next to him. Bill knows it is wrong. He knows that in America child dealers kill each other in the playgrounds and thirteen-year-old girls sell their bodies for crack. He has done an immoral thing because he felt guilty about not taking the children to Disneyland all those years ago. And because he thought he could cheat death.

Of course, he is rather enjoying flying again.

He wants to ask Dwayne if the drugs will be sold in playgrounds. He does not quite know how to ask. Of course he can't just come out with it.

"Dwayne," Bill says.

"Yup."

"The — uh — cargo."

"The cargo," Dwayne says, no inflection.

"Where is it destined for?"

"We're going to the Valhalla Motel in Lonesome Snapper," Dwayne says. "You know that."

"I know that," Bill says. "I just meant — I didn't want names. I…"

"You wanted to know in general where it's destined for?" the American asks.

That's it. "In general terms. Yes," Bill says.

"It's destined for recreational use," Dwayne says.

"Recreational use," Bill says. Recreational use?

"It's grass," Dwayne says.

"Oh." Bill is surprised.

"Marijuana," Dwayne explains.

Bill already knows grass is slang for marijuana. He may be old but he's not stupid.

"You thought it was coke?" Dwayne asks.

"I'm rather afraid I did," Bill admits.

"The big boys wouldn't let me into that," Dwayne says. "I'm strictly small-time. Not enough working capital. Not enough contacts."

"I suppose," Bill essays, "if you had more money this arrangement…" He waves his hand around the plane.

"I would've hired a pro," Dwayne says. "No offence."

"None taken," Bill says.

This strange American is surprisingly easy to talk to. "Is marijuana addictive?" Bill asks.

**(8)**

By day the artificial turf in the Miami stadium looks an unnatural green. But in the moonlight now it looks a shiny black. Zeke's big hands cradle the ball on the artificial turf, the laces facing away from the kicker. Keith makes his run from the side, measuring his steps, long and strong. Keith turns as he kicks, putting the full force of boot and leg into the ball, following through flawlessly. And then he stands and watches, fists held up before him in prayer, looking into the round moon shining over the rim of the stadium behind the goal posts. The ball tumbles end over end, and it's through. The kick is good.

Keith throws his hands above his head in the touchdown sign. Zeke stands up. They both wear pink uniforms, Florida Flamingoes uniforms, identical, both with the number 11, Zeke's number. For Zeke plays quarterback for the Flamingoes. He has snuck Keith into the dressing room, into the stadium, and held the ball while Keith achieved his deepest wish. And now they hug in the moonlight, one man with two backs, and on each back the number 11.

**(9)**

Sam Rollins is shucking nuts at the Valhalla Motel. A pile of peanut husks overflows the ashtray. Sam has a brown paper bag of nuts by his feet. He crunches along, bored out of his mind. One thing about Sam's job, there's too much waiting.

"Can I go to the toilet?" Claire asks.

"You already been to the bathroom," Sam says.

"I have to go again," she says in a whiny voice.

"OK," Sam says. She goes. Sam grabs another nut. The phone rings.

They all freeze. It rings again. Sam's gun is in his hand. Mark, on the bed, is nearest the phone.

"Take it. And no funny stuff or I blow your buddy's balls off," Sam says to Mark. "If he has any," he adds as an afterthought.

Sam's colleagues Tony and Carlos laugh dutifully.

Mark does not laugh. He leans across to take the phone. Sam is right there with him, kneeling by the bed next to the aquamarine princess phone, the barrel of his gun inches from Mark's temple. Babur sits next to Mark on the bed. Tony and Carlos watch. Claire appears at the bathroom door.

"Hello," Mark says.

"Mark?" a woman says.

"Martha," Mark says. It's the obsessive.

Babur almost jumps. "Martha?"

Sam Rollins takes a miniaturized listening device from his shirt pocket and gently attaches its sucker to the phone. A thin cord leads to Sam's earpiece. He nods to Mark.

"I just had to call you," Martha says.

"Yes," Mark says.

"I've been waking up all night every night covered in sweat, just the whole bed dripping in it. And I can hardly stand the smell, I'm so ashamed in the mornings. And I've been running to the toilet, five times yesterday, five times, really bad. I'm sort of ashamed of that too, and now I've got this sort of a rash on my arms, all kinds of hard bumps. I think they're sort of purple, like it says in the book."

Babur has figured it out. "You gave her the number," he

says to Mark.

Mark puts his hand over the mouthpiece. "I left the address on her answering machine. I think she got the number from directory enquiries," he whispers.

"Same thing," Babur says.

"Does that sound like AIDS to you?" Martha asks.

Of course it sounds like AIDS, Sam Rollins thinks. Poor woman.

"No," Mark says. "It sounds like anxiety to me."

Rollins is surprised.

"Our bloody holiday," Babur hisses into Mark's other ear, "and you have to give some loon your number."

Mark flaps a hand at Babur, shooing him away. "What have you been worrying about?" Mark says into the phone.

"AIDS," Martha says.

Rollins figures that's obvious.

"No, I mean what else have you been thinking about?" Mark says.

Babur is sitting a little apart from Mark, looking pissed off. "She's not the only obsessive around here," he mutters.

"Shut up," Rollins mouths at Babur. Rollins wants to hear what the woman has to say.

"Brendan," Martha says.

"Brendan," Mark says. It's not a question, he just repeats the word. Rollins understands that Mark is some sort of shrink. He has never actually heard anybody being shrunk before.

"My, he was, the man who, the one who gave it to me," Martha says.

"The man you made love with," Mark says.

"The man I made love with," Martha says, without inflection.

Neither of them talks for a moment. Sam Rollins wonders about Laura Smolensky.

"Martha," Mark says.

"Yes."

"How was it?" Mark asks.

"How was what?" she says.

"When you had sex with him, Martha, how was it?"

There is a long silence at the other end of the phone.

"It was wonderful," Martha says. "Absolutely wonderful."

There is another silence.

"Best sex I ever had," she says. She giggles.

There is a long gap.

"How do you feel about that?" Mark asks.

"Guilty, of course," Martha says.

Martha finally hangs up. Sam says to Mark, "C'mere." He leads Mark into the bathroom.

Sam sits on the edge of the bath. He gestures with the gun for Mark to sit on the toilet seat.

"Sorry about the gun," Sam says.

"That's OK," Mark says. He sits nervously.

"You seem to be sort of an expert on this kind of thing," Sam says.

"This thing."

"The AIDS thing," Sam says.

"Yes. Yes, I am."

"Could you tell me, I don't want to take up too much of your time..."

"It's OK," Mark says.

"Let me put a sort of a hypothetical situation for you. There's this guy, see, he thinks he's pretty street-smart, but sometimes these things happen, he's not so sure, and he wonders, can he really tell about this one particular girl, who he really likes her, but you can't tell by looking, can you?"

"Why don't you tell me what's worrying you," Mark says. He is on automatic pilot.

"This isn't too easy for me," Sam says.

"I know," Mark says.

"I know this girl, see. She seems like a nice girl, you know. Hell, nobody's a virgin these days, am I right? I'm not, you're not, these days the Blessed Mother, she came back, she'd be going down on guys right, left and centre. So who are we to judge? Right?"

"Mm," Mark says.

"So these days you take your chances," Sam says. "I go out in the rain too, like everybody else, but I wear my galoshes, you know what I mean?"

"Yes." Mark is bored out of his mind.

"But this girl, this woman, she's a woman, Laura, when we make love she puts her" — he holds up a finger — "straight up my asshole. Bam!"

"Yes," Mark says.

"Is that dangerous?"

"No," Mark says.

"You sure?"

"Yes."

"Why do you think she does it?" Sam asks.

"I don't know. Could be a lot of reasons. What do you think?" Mark says.

Sam goes to the heart of the problem. "What I mean is, where do you think she learned that?"

## *(10)*

It is dark. Bill is in the middle of the night sky, flying without lights. The moon has gone down. Only the dashboard glows. It all looks beautiful to Bill. But it sounds like there is something wrong with John's breathing.

Bill turns his head and says over his shoulder, "Paul?"

"Yes." A quiet voice.

"Is he all right?"

"He's sleeping," Paul whispers.

Andy and John are on an ice field in Zanskar now, toiling slowly up toward the monastery. It looks like the Potala in Lhasa, with its endless storeys and narrow windows high up. Crows sit on the windowsills. The monastery is on a cliff, and sometimes the ice field moves underneath them.

"I'm cold," Andy says. He's doing pretty well for a puppet.

"Not long now," John says. He is having trouble with his breathing.

Andy reaches up for his big friend's hand. "Dad's here," Andy says.

In Zanskar?

"In wherever," Andy says. "Dad loves you."

"I know," John says. Up here his lungs rasp with the altitude. Not much further now, and the whole long journey will be over.

"Do you love Dad?" Andy asks.

John does not like this question.

"I don't think I love anybody any more," John says. The ice growls under his feet. Breathing hurts now. From the monastery above comes the deep bass peace of the great musical horns. Vultures circle above the ice.

"Do you love me?" Andy asks, looking up at him.

"Of course I love you," John says.

"Fat lot of good that does," Andy says. "I'm only a fucking puppet."

Beneath their feet the ice starts to scream.

**(11)**

In the motel room the phone rings again an hour later. Mark answers it. "Yes?"

"Mark?" Martha says.

"Yes."

"I've been thinking about it. You were right. It wasn't AIDS at all. It was sex I was worrying about. I know I shouldn't talk like this, but Brendan was the best fuck I ever had, and I guess I've just been feeling guilty towards my family for enjoying it."

"Right," Mark says.

"Guilt never did anybody any good, did it?" she asks across three thousand miles.

"Guilt's a pile of shit," Mark says.

"Thank you," she says.

"You're welcome," Mark says. He means it.

"I just called to say thank you," Martha says.

"You're welcome," Mark says.

"Well," Martha says. "Bye."

"Bye," Mark says.

"Thanks," she says, and hangs up.

Mark turns to Babur and shrugs his shoulders.

"I love you anyway," Babur says.

There is a sharp rap on the door. Sam Rollins covers the door with his gun. Carlos slowly turns the handle and opens the door.

It's one of the other agents. He has a gun trained on Keith and a large, nervous man Mark has never seen before.

"Jesus Christ Superstud," Sam Rollins says, "Zeke Elliot."

After she hangs up on Mark, Martha takes a deep breath and dials a London number. A man answers: "Hello?"

"Brendan?" Martha says.

"Martha," Brendan says, his voice rich and warm, "long time, no see."

**(12)**

"Down there," Dwayne says. They are flying over Lonesome Snapper.

Bill looks. He can see car headlights a few hundred feet below. He banks to come back. John and Paul are holding hands in the back seat.

"Are you all right?" Dwayne says to somebody.

Nobody answers.

"Are you OK?" Dwayne says again. Bill is coming out of his turn.

"What's wrong, Dad?" John says.

Bill realizes he is shaking.

"Landing," Bill says to John.

"You ever done this sort of thing before?" Dwayne asks.

"Oh, yes," Bill says. He gives a high laugh.

"What is it, Dad?" John says.

Bill decides now is the time to explain to his son. He starts. "The last time I landed we were hit. It was a crash landing." He stops. John waits.

"How did it turn out?" Dwayne says.

"Not good," Bill says. He has overshot the landing strip again. He starts to turn.

John undoes his seat belt and leans forward. "What happened, Dad?" he asks quietly. His chin is almost resting on his father's shoulder.

"Everybody else died," Bill says.

"Fuck," Dwayne shouts.

"Sorry," Bill says.

Dwayne, more controlled now, asks Bill, "Was it your fault?"

"The court martial exonerated me," Bill says. They are still turning into the wind. Easy does it.

John says, "Did you forgive yourself, Dad?"

"You never forgive yourself for something like that," Bill says. This time he's going for it. The plane's nose points down.

Dwayne clenches his seat, swearing almost silently.

The plane points steeply down. The dark ground rushes up at them.

Paul crushes John's hand in his.

And they're down. It's a perfect landing.

"Christ," Dwayne says.

Bill sits there a moment. He opens the plane door and drops to the ground. He feels good. Somebody sticks a gun in his face.

*(13)*

Carlos and Tony take them out of the plane and up to the motel without any trouble. They brought them back to the motel. Sam meets them there and Dwayne says, "Aw, fuck. Sam Rollins."

"Hi, Dwayne," Sam says.

Sam leaves Tony to guard the civilians in the motel room. Then Sam Rollins and Carlos take Dwayne and Zeke and Keith into the next room.

Keith does not understand why they are going into the next room. He watches the others. They sit down confidently. His Zeke and that Sam and the Dwayne in the green tie all know what they're doing.

It turns out they're going to deal. Sam wants the plane and all the coke in it and Dwayne and the rest can fuck off and die for all he cares.

Dwayne says no way. He has a living to make. He's spent years building an adequate capital base. Sam can have half the coke and none of the plane. The plane's on loan from a friend, and Dwayne could not bear it if his friend ceased to be a friend. Dwayne mentions a name.

"I see what you mean," Sam Rollins says.

Each man sticks to his bargaining position. Carlos, Sam's sidekick, strokes his gun barrel. Zeke seems relaxed. Everybody ignores Keith. He can't imagine what he and Zeke are doing here. He finds out.

"No," Dwayne says. "Be fair."

"I am fair," Sam Rollins says.

"Of course *you're* fair," Dwayne says. "But all the coke *and* the plane, that's not fair."

Sam Rollins smiles a grim little smile. His head turns to looks at Zeke. Zeke has his big hands spread on his knees.

"Zeke?" Sam says.

"Yeah?" Zeke says, his voice deep and slow.

"Could you get my kid to be a water boy for home games?" Sam Rollins asks.

"Your little boy?" Zeke asks.

"Yes."

"How old?" Zeke says.

"Eleven," Sam says. He sounds proud.

"Maybe," Zeke says.

Sam Rollins turns to Dwayne. "I take half the coke and my boy gets to be water boy for the Flamingoes and sit on the bench."

"OK," Dwayne says. He looks to Zeke.

"OK," Zeke says.

"Every home game," Sam says.

"Every home game," Zeke agrees.

Sam Rollins and Dwayne and Carlos go out to the plane to split the coke. Sam is happy fit to burst. Now Sam Junior will have to love him.

# *Chapter 5*

While the deal goes down the rest of them wait next door. Mark and Babur sit together at the head of the bed, holding hands, looking stunned.

John is stretched out across the floor by the bed. Paul sits on the floor by the bathroom door. That way his head is right next to John's, and they can talk quietly.

Bill and Claire sit on the floor near the door. Tony the guard stands by the door. Bill leans back against the bed by John's feet. Bill is tired. The bedspread is light, ribbed, with little tassels on the bottom. Bill's fingers play with one of the tassels. He has destroyed everybody's life, in ways he did not understand, but should have anticipated.

"I'm sorry," Paul says quietly to John. "I should never have left you."

"You didn't leave me," John says. "I drove you away."

"I find it hard to live with myself now," Paul says.

John does not respond.

"You shouldn't leave somebody when you find out they have HIV," Paul says.

"Don't be a horse's ass," John says, breath exploding. He struggles to control his lungs. "I asked you to leave, Paulie."

"I left," Paul says. For him it's that simple.

"Would you have gone if I asked you to stay?" John says.

For a while Paul says nothing. "No." He thinks it over some more. "No."

John is wheezing.

"I've killed you by bringing you here," Paul says, almost whispering.

"No," John says.

"I should have let you go to Tibet," Paul says.

"You haven't killed me."

"Don't try to take care of my feelings, Johnny," Paul says.

"I was going to die anyway," John says.

"You can't say that."

"I'm going to die. Stop denying it."

Paul thinks about it. "Denial's a sort of love."

John nods, then shrugs his shoulders. "Sometimes it's just a way of living," he says. His breathing seems a bit better to Paul.

"You wanted to go to Tibet. That's what you really wanted."

"I wanted to die alone," John says.

Bill and Claire have been listening. Bill notices Claire's hand digging into his wrist. He says to his daughter, very quietly, "Do you think we made him so ill bringing him here that he's going to die?"

"It doesn't matter," Claire says.

It matters to Bill. "Did I?" he says.

"Yes," Claire says.

Bill brings his hands up to cover his face.

"It doesn't matter," Claire says.

That makes no sense to Bill. "What do you mean?" he says.

"It doesn't matter," she says. "It truly does not matter."

Paul says, "Why did you ask me to leave?"

"I couldn't ask you to stay," John says.

"Why not?" Paul says quickly.

"Because..." John starts, and Paul realizes why and cuts him off.

"That's OK. I understand," Paul says.

John searches Paul's face. Paul does understand. "Why did you go?" John says.

"Because you were being such a prick."

"I had HIV," John says.

"So?" Paul says.

"I was denying I had it."

"You wanted to die alone," Paul says.

"I thought I'd given it to you," John says.

"I thought I'd given it to you," Paul says.

"Snap," John says. They smile.

John asks, "Why didn't you tell me about the test?"

"Guilt. For surviving."

"I was a pig," John says.

"Yes."

"I couldn't ask anybody to love me," John says.

"No," Paul says.

"Not if I was going to die."

"No," Paul says.

"I was a jerk," John says.

"You were just frightened," Paul says. "So was I."

"Are you frightened now?" John asks.

Paul thinks that one over. "No."

"I am," John says.

Paul gets up off the floor and sits on the bed. He lifts John's head and cradles it in his lap.

Bill watches Paul and his son. Bill is shaking now, feeling convulsing his body, crying for all his remembered dead.

John is at rest on Paul's lap. Neither has spoken for some time. Paul strokes John's forehead. John's eyes are open.

"Paulie," John says.

"Still frightened, Johnny?" Paul says.

"Scared stiff."

"Can you say it?" Paul asks.

"Say what?"

"I need you," Paul says.

"I love you," John says.

"No, Johnny," Paul says. "Say: I need you."

John looks up at the grey eyes so far away. "I need you, Paulie," he says.

Paul raises his lover's head and lowers his own lips as they kiss, Paul taking the weight of John's body, and then John straining upwards with new strength to consume Paul, to tear his soul out through his mouth.

Paul and John stop to breathe. The room is quiet. Everybody is looking at them. The guard with the gun has gone and Keith and a big man are there.

Keith explains the deal. It takes them all some time to understand it. Finally they do.

John says, "Let's go to Disneyland."

They went next morning. Zeke and Dwayne came too. They got a wheelchair for John: he was tired. A lot of Mickeys and

Goofys recognized John's condition and were especially kind to him. Andy the Mouse got pretty manic and spent half an hour talking shop with a Mickey. He was overwhelmed with joy. And the halls of plastic America rang with the laughter of heroes.

That day was the climax. John lived another twenty-seven months. Sometimes it felt like an anti-climax, and his friends didn't know what to do with him. But Paul figured John had always been a stubborn bastard, and loved him.